Alison Roberts is a New Zealander, currently lucky enough to be living in the south of France. She is also lucky enough to write for the Mills & Boon Medical Romance line. A primary school teacher in a former life, she is now a qualified paramedic. She loves to travel and dance, drink champagne, and spend time with her daughter and her friends.

THE DOCTOR'S WIFE FOR KEEPS

ALISON ROBERTS

MILLS & BOON

First published in Great Britain 2018
by Mills & Boon, an imprint of HarperCollins*Publishers*
1 London Bridge Street, London, SE1 9GF

Large Print edition 2018

© 2018 Alison Roberts

ISBN: 978-0-263-07289-1

MIX
Paper from
responsible sources
FSC™ C007454

This book is produced from independently certified
FSC™ paper to ensure responsible forest management. For
more information visit www.harpercollins.co.uk/green.

Printed and bound in Great Britain
by CPI Group (UK) Ltd, Croydon, CR0 4YY

For Sarah, Luke and Brendan,
with lots of love and very fond memories
of our adventures in the Czech Republic. xx

PROLOGUE

'I THINK WE'RE LOST.'

Kate Saunders slowed the SUV she was driving to take another hairpin bend on this alpine road that seemed to be going on for ever and getting narrower as the tall forest pressed in on both sides. She glanced sideways at her companion—her best friend and flatmate, Georgia.

'Whose bright idea was it to enter this international medical rescue competition? Oh, yeah... *yours...*'

'It's an adventure.' Georgia was grinning. 'Admit it—you're loving it already.'

Kate snorted, tipping her head a little to ease the crick in her neck. 'Road trips always sound more fun than they actually are. It's a hell of a long way from Scotland to the back of beyond in the Czech Republic. I've never even heard of the town we're trying to find.'

'Rakovi. It's a ski resort. And this is the biggest competition of its kind in the world. I've been hearing about it for years—ever since I became a paramedic.'

'Well, I've never heard of it.'

'That's because you're a doctor and your lot aren't as adventurous.'

'Hmm…' There was some truth in that. Kate had been focused on her career from the moment she'd been accepted for medical school at the age of twenty two. Georgia had helped her celebrate her thirty-fifth birthday a few months ago and her idea of a gift had been to enter her in this competition as a doctor/paramedic team. She had already booked accommodation in London and Germany to break up the travel and, probably thanks to the bottle of excellent champagne they were sharing, it had seemed like a brilliant idea at the time.

Now she wasn't so sure.

'Have we even got out of Poland yet?'

'Ages ago. It's not far now.'

'We don't want to be late for registration.'

'Don't stress. They've got a couple of hundred teams from about twenty different countries to process. If we're a bit late it'll just mean we don't have to queue for so long.'

Kate slowed again to cross a narrow bridge over a tumbling mountain stream. 'I can't believe we're competing in such a huge field.'

'It's broken up into categories, remember. There'll be paramedic teams with their ambulances from all over Europe. I can't wait till the end where everybody drives in convoy around all the local villages with their lights and sirens on. I've heard it's a memorable experience. Then there are the doctors and medical student teams and other combinations. I just hope there's enough like us to give us our own category, otherwise we'll be competing against teams that have up to four members.'

'I just hope I don't make an idiot of myself. I'm a paediatrician, Georgie. I work in a nice, safe hospital with any amount of resources and backup. You would have been better to pick an emergency specialist.'

'You do plenty of emergency work. And you've lived with me long enough to qualify as an honorary paramedic. You've even been out on the road with me a few times. You'll be brilliant and who cares if we don't win? We're here to have fun, remember? To have an adventure and meet lots of new people and...' Georgia's grin was decidedly mischievous now. 'We're both single and gorgeous. Have you thought about how many men there are going to be at this thing?'

'Georgie...' Kate shook her head. 'You never give up, do you? You've only just got over the last disaster and you're ready to do it again?'

'Oh, I have no intention of falling for someone. What's that saying? The best way to get over a man is to get under another one?'

Kate had to laugh. And she had to admire Georgia's resilience. At least she kept trying and Kate hadn't even done that for quite some time. It was so disheartening when a relationship failed to live up to expectations and the goalposts of true love and that dream family and children of her own got shifted a little further away yet again.

'Casual sex has never appealed to me.'

'Yeah…you're so old school, Kate. An ultimate romantic. You really believe that you're going to see 'the one' across a crowded room and it'll be love at first sight and a happy-ever-after with a few bluebirds fluttering over the carpet of rose petals and…'

'Oh, stop it,' Kate growled. Her friend's tone was teasing but, disturbingly, there was an element of truth in the scene. Not the bluebirds, of course. Or the rose petals.

But, yeah…she did believe that 'the one' was out there somewhere and that happy-ever-afters were quite possible for the lucky few. And who knew? It wasn't beyond the realms of possibility that *he* might be amongst this huge, random gathering of people with a common interest.

A flicker of excitement that had nothing to do with the adventure of competing lifted her spirits noticeably. And with that flicker came a rush of affection for her friend. Poor Georgia had been through the mill when it came to men so it was no wonder she was a little on the bitter side at the moment.

'Just be careful, hon. Okay?'

'Of course.'

Kate had seen that innocent look before. It meant that she was hiding something.

'You have given up on that hare-brained scheme you came up with after that bastard, Rick, walked out, haven't you?'

'I have no idea what you're talking about.'

'Oh, yes, you do. The one where you gave up on men completely and were going to have a baby all by yourself?' As much as Kate adored children, she couldn't imagine choosing to have a family on her own. The whole package was the goal and there was a proper order to do it in. You fell in love, got married and *then* had a baby. Georgia was only a year older than she was. They still had time…didn't they?

'Well, obviously I haven't given up on men *completely*. And I'm over Rick. He's ancient history—like all the others. Ooh, look…a signpost. We're only fifteen kilometres away.'

That flicker of excitement ignited into a small but steady flame. Kate hadn't given up on men completely either and maybe fate, in the form of Georgia's determination, had pushed her in the direction of this competition for a reason.

'Halleluiah.' Kate grinned at her friend. 'The end is in sight.'

'Nah…the *beginning* is in sight.' Georgia stretched her arms above her head and gave a whoop. 'Bring it on.'

CHAPTER ONE

NO WAY...

It *couldn't* be...

'Come on, Kate. You can get your T-shirt later. We need to register and then find our room.'

A firm nudge made Kate turn her head and start moving again. 'Sorry... I thought I saw someone I knew.'

'Who?'

'Luke. Luke Anderson. An old friend. We went through med school together.'

'Hmm...' Georgia was scanning the queues in front of a line of desks. 'Can you see what's on that sign?'

'The desks are divided into alphabetic sections according to the country the team is representing. "S" is over there.' This time it was Kate leading the way. She approved of such disciplined organisation and it boded well for a smoothly run competition. The people behind the desks were looking weary. How many hundreds of people had they processed already? There was still a queue in front of the section that included 'S'.

Kate looked around at the sea of people, many of whom were in the uniforms of their ambulance organisation, with bright orange or red overalls and jackets. It was noisy and she could hear languages she couldn't identify. A lot of people seemed to know each other very well and enthusiastic greetings added to the aura of controlled chaos. At least she had a few minutes to take it all in as they waited their turn.

'So…this Luke…' Georgia raised an eyebrow. 'Is he good looking?'

'I guess…' Kate tried to recapture that fleeting glance to decide whether it was possible she had really seen him. 'Very tall. Dark hair. Brown eyes.'

'Oh… I *love* brown eyes. My favourite.'

Kate's breath came out in a huff. They were both women in their mid-thirties. Independent and successful. Were they really having a conversation that made them sound like boy-mad teenagers?

'I haven't seen him for five years. Since he got married.'

'Oh…' The tone was very different this time. Georgia's interest had evaporated.

For some reason that annoyed Kate. 'We were really good friends. We lost touch because his wife couldn't handle him having a female friend. I'd love to catch up. I don't even know what part of the world he's living in now. But he's a paediatric surgeon so it's pretty unlikely he'd come to something like this.'

'I'll bet he'd say the same thing if he thought he'd seen you.'

Kate couldn't argue with that. Not that there was any more time to even think about it because they'd reached the front of the queue. There were folders of documents to collect that included detailed instructions and maps. They received large identification numbers that they would have to wear pinned to their clothing at all times and coloured wristbands that were clipped on.

'These numbers go on your vehicle.' The official's English was excellent but heavily accented. 'These are your vouchers for meals and this is your room number. Go to the accommodation block and they will show you where to go. Don't forget the welcome ceremony and briefing at nineteen hundred hours. If you hurry, you should have time for a meal first.'

The ski resort sprawled over several levels on the steep hillside with a road that separated each level in a zigzag. A road that was jam packed with vehicles parked on both sides of it. The variety of colours was amazing. Red and white predominated but there were yellow and green emergency vehicles with various designs of reflective stripes and insignia. Amongst the dozens of ambulances and marked emergency Jeeps and SUVs—many of which were also decorated with flags and other accessories, Georgia's car looked small and plain. And it was parked far enough away to make it a mission to collect their bags.

'You've got a Scottish flag, haven't you?'

'Och, aye...' Georgia nodded. 'One for each front window. And a bagpipe-playing bear that we can attach to the front bumper. We can do that later, though. I'm *starving*...'

'I'll just put the vehicle number stickers on. It was one at the front and one at the back, wasn't it? Did they say which part of the windscreen it should go on?'

Georgia shook her head. 'Just make it visible. You can read the rules later.'

Kate frowned. 'I'll just put the front one on the dashboard for now. If we stick it in the wrong place, it might not come off.'

Georgia paused in her task of hauling their bags from the back to give Kate a loaded glance.

'You know, sometimes you make me feel like I'm out with my mother.'

'If it keeps you out of trouble then that's a good thing.'

'I'm a big girl, Kate. I *can* look after myself.' But Georgia was smiling now. 'It's a good thing you're here, though. We certainly won't get eliminated for breaking any rules. And, hey…how good is it that we've got our own category? There must be at least five other teams that have a doctor and one or two paramedics with them. Maybe one of them includes your friend.'

Kate pulled out the handle of her bag and started wheeling it down the road.

'Doubt it. It must have just been someone who looked a bit like him. I've seen a dozen tall men with dark hair since then.'

Because she'd been looking?

She was still looking, she realised as they lined up and presented their meal vouchers in exchange for a plate laden with stew and dumplings. There was a bar open in the dining area and many tables had people enjoying a beer or wine with their meals. So many tables. So many people.

She'd already decided Luke couldn't possibly be here so why was she scanning the room so carefully now?

'There's some space on that table.' Georgia led the way. 'Do you mind if we join you guys?'

'Please do.' The man's face lit up beneath sun-streaked blond hair as he looked at Georgia. 'I'm Dave. This is Ken and that's Sally, who's stuffing her face there.'

'You're from Australia, right?'

'No. New Zealand.' Dave sighed heavily. 'Everybody thinks our accent is the same but it really isn't.' He grinned at Georgia. 'No mistaking yours. You're Scottish.'

'I am. I like your uniforms. Are you paramedics?'

'Yeah… You guys?'

'I'm a paramedic. Kate's a doctor. Is this your first time here?'

'Sure is. Never seen anything like it.'

'Where are you based at home? City or country?'

'Auckland. Biggest city in the country. And up there in the top cities of the world to live in. You should come and visit sometime.'

'Oh? What's so great about Auckland?'

The conversation, as they swapped details about their home towns and talked about how little they knew of what was to happen tomorrow, was lively but Kate was only half listening.

Why was it so unsettling, she wondered, to be disappointed that she'd made a mistake? It wasn't as if Luke had ever been anything more than a friend.

On his side, anyway.

On her side, too, after she'd got over that silly crush. And it hadn't been that hard, had it?

Humiliating, maybe, when she'd felt invisible as anything more than a friend, but they had been very good friends and that was something special. Something that often lasted way longer than any romantic relationships. They'd studied together, competed fiercely to see could get better marks in exams and had supported each other in those first, nerve-racking encounters with real patients in real hospitals.

They'd kept in touch all through those early years of their careers after medical school, even though they'd ended up in different cities and she'd convinced herself that she was genuinely delighted when he'd fallen head over heels in love with the gorgeous Nadia—a nurse he'd met in his first year as a surgical registrar. She hadn't been the one for Luke but she'd cared enough about him to wish him complete happiness with the woman who'd been lucky enough to be chosen.

Okay, it had been more than a little hurtful when contact had ceased but she'd always hoped that, one day, when Nadia felt more secure, the friendship would somehow be rekindled. A hope that had been slowly evaporating over the years, however. She hadn't even thought about Luke for quite a long time. Until she'd thought she'd spotted him…

Maybe, when she got home, she'd find out where he was working these days. Drop him an email, even, and just say hi.

The plan was satisfying enough to enable her to put the distraction firmly to one side and tune in properly to the conversation around her. New Zealand was a place that had always fascinated her and she was keen to hear about what it was like to live and work there.

By the time she followed the others to get to the

welcome ceremony and briefing, she had completely forgotten about Luke Anderson. It was taking more than enough concentration not to lose sight of Georgia or their new friends as they squeezed into a very crowded room.

'Excuse me…' She had to turn sideways to get past a group of medics wearing heavy coats with fluorescent stripes and rescue insignia. They were big men and maybe they hadn't heard her because one of them stepped back and pushed Kate into the person on the other side of the space she'd been trying to get through. She felt hands grip her arms as someone tried to prevent her falling.

'Oh, I'm so sorry.' Kate could feel her face reddening as she regained her balance.

'No problem. It's a bit of a squeeze in here, isn't it?'

Kate's jaw dropped as she lifted her head. She knew that voice *so* well…

'Oh, my God… *Kate?*'

A huge, dumb grin was spreading over her face but words had deserted her. Not that she needed them for a moment because Luke had enveloped her in a hug that was making it difficult to take a breath.

'Kate?'

The voice came from behind her and she turned as the tight hold loosened.

'Oh, thank goodness. I thought I'd lost you.'

'Georgie…this is my friend, Luke…'

Someone was tapping on a microphone, which triggered a screech of feedback that made people groan.

'Sorry about that but welcome, everybody… If we could have a bit of quiet, please?'

Kate shut up immediately but Luke didn't appear to have heard the request.

'What on earth are you doing here?'

'It was a birthday present,' she muttered. 'Long story…'

'*Shh,*' someone behind her hissed. 'We're trying to listen.'

Luke made an apologetic grimace but then winked at Kate.

'Later,' he mouthed, turning to peer over the heads of others to see who was speaking.

Kate started listening, too. After the welcome speech and a list of how many countries were participating, another speaker got up to share important information.

'Between eleven-thirty and midnight tonight, you will all receive your list of events. You will be given the GPS coordinates of the scenario and a start time. Please be there at least ten minutes before that time. If you are late, you will not be admitted and you will not be marked in that section of the competition.'

Georgia elbowed Kate. 'No chance of that happening,' she whispered. 'Not when I'm with you.'

The dig at her compulsion to follow directions to the letter failed to bother Kate. How could it when she was feeling so unexpectedly good?

She had Luke standing on her other side and, every so often, they glanced sideways—apparently at the exact same moment—to catch each other's gaze. And every time it happened, the feeling got stronger.

It was like going home. Or back to a beloved place, like where you'd had your summer holidays all through childhood. A feeling of something so familiar you could relax completely. Of something that had the promise of delivering the same good things it always had.

And, yes…there was something more.

A flicker of that initial crush, perhaps? A realisation that none of her own relationships had ever worked well enough because that flicker had never been fanned into something that had felt as meaningful as even her friendship with Luke had been?

'The rally covers a period of twenty-four hours and you will have both a daytime and a night-time section. There will be twelve tasks for you to complete but there will be breaks in your schedule during which you can take meals or have a rest.

Time to catch up properly with an old friend, perhaps? The feeling of anticipation took on a softer edge for Kate. A warm glow, even.

There were pictures on a big screen on the wall

now. There was a map of the local area as an official explained how far they might have to travel to get to some of the scenarios and what local landmarks and hazards to watch out for.

Finally, there were reminders of the rules.

'The competition is held in English. All instructions will be in this language and your patients are fluent enough to answer any relevant questions. The officials grading your performance will also be doing this in English and teams will be marked down for communication in any other language.'

Kate caught Luke's eye again. Surely that gave them a distinct advantage over many of the teams here? For the first time, she could feel a kick of a desire to do well. To win, even?

Maybe that was down to the gleam she'd caught in Luke's gaze. They'd always set out to see who could better the other. And then they would always celebrate the winner without any suggestion of animosity. With a dollop of pride, even…

'And while we're on the subject of communication,' the official continued, 'it is forbidden for any team to discuss the scenarios with other teams until the competition is finished so please be careful. Anyone found to be using information they have received in advance will be eliminated.'

'What section are you in?' she asked as soon as the formalities were over. 'All doctors? Doctors and med students?'

'Doctor/paramedic.' Luke put his arm around the man standing beside him. 'This is Matteo Martini. Italian paramedic extraordinaire.'

'Ooh…' Georgia had moved closer. 'A martini? Yes, please… Extra-dry—with an olive.'

They all laughed. 'This is Georgie,' Kate said. 'My paramedic partner.'

She caught Luke's gaze again and this time the gleam took her right back to her student days. Standing in line outside an examination room with both of them knowing how hard they'd studied and both of them determined to be top of the class.

It had become a joke amongst their fellow students about whose turn it was to come first because they were such an equal match. There was never much of a gap between their marks.

'My turn, I think.' Kate grinned.

'I don't think so.' But then Luke frowned. 'Who got first last time? Good grief…it's so long ago, I can't even remember.'

'Finals,' Kate growled. 'And it was you.' She was scowling at him now. 'You don't need to look so smug about it.'

Luke adjusted his face. 'It was a long time ago.'

'Mmm.' Kate held his gaze. 'Too long.'

They were being herded out of the room now. A glance over her shoulder showed Kate that Georgia and Matteo were following so they went with the flow. It seemed that everybody was heading for the bar to wait until their scenario list and start times were handed out.

'So how *are* you?' Kate had to raise her voice to be heard over the babble of so many languages around them. 'I haven't seen you since your wedding.'

'I know. I'm sorry…' There was something in Luke's expression that suggested he was sorry for more than the lack of contact. 'Can I get you a drink?'

'Just a soda water,' Kate said. 'I need to keep a clear head for tomorrow.'

'Beer for me,' Matteo said. 'Georgie?'

The mischievous expression on Georgia's face made Kate suppress a sigh. It was clear she was enjoying the handsome Italian's company but surely she wasn't going to be obvious enough ask for a martini? The sigh came out as one of relief as Georgia spoke.

'White wine,' she said. 'Sparkling, if they've got it. I do love a bit of sparkle.'

Matteo raised an eyebrow. 'A taste for champagne, yes? Classy...' He went to help Luke carry the drinks while the girls found a place to sit down.

'You want me to take Matteo somewhere else?' Georgia asked. 'So that you and Luke can have some alone time?'

'Don't be daft.' The words came out sounding more irritated than Kate had intended. 'We're friends. Or we were. It's so long since I've seen him that we're practically strangers now.'

She averted her gaze as she finished her sentence. It was so far from the truth. But she couldn't admit to Georgia how it made her feel to see Luke again. She hadn't quite got her own head around it yet.

It seemed that Luke had followed her example and got a non-alcoholic drink for himself as well. Clearly he wanted to be as competitive as possible tomorrow as well. Kate had to hide a smile as they touched glasses.

Game on...

'Cheers,' she said. 'I have to say, you're probably the last person I would have expected to run into here. Have you changed specialties and gone into emergency medicine?'

'No. I'm still a paediatric surgeon but I do specialise in trauma cases. It's Matt's fault I'm here.'

'Snap,' Kate told him. 'Georgia entered me as a birthday present. She said I needed some adventure in my life.'

'And do you?' There was a question in Luke's eyes that went far deeper than the amused query.

Was her life going the way she had planned it out so carefully? Was she happy?

She was saved having to find an answer by Georgia leaning closer. 'So how do you two boys know each other?'

'I did a stint in a hospital in Milan,' Luke told her. 'I got lost one day trying to find my apartment and this ambulance pulled up beside me. Matt was driving.'

'I'd seen him in the emergency department of the hospital,' Matteo put in. 'I'd stayed with a child I'd brought in who'd been hit by a car and Luke had been called for a surgical consultation.'

'He gave me a ride home,' Luke continued. 'And then he said he'd pick me up again after he finished his shift because he knew where the best beer in Milan was.'

'Italy,' Kate breathed. 'How exciting. Did Nadia love living there?'

Matteo was staring at Luke. 'Who's Nadia?'

'My ex-wife.'

'Ah…the cheating cow?'

'That's the one.'

It was Kate's turn to stare at Luke. 'Oh, my God…you and Nadia split up?'

Luke was eyeing Matteo's beer as if he was regretting his decision on drinks. 'Yep.'

'But…'

Everybody turned to stare at *her* and Kate bit her lip. 'Sorry,' she muttered. 'It's just that you guys were so in love…'

Luke snorted. 'Yeah…well, I won't be making that mistake again, believe *me*.'

'It kind of cures you,' Matteo offered. 'When the wife you love turns out to have been shagging every other man she met. I'm with Luke on this one. If someone cheated on me or lied to me like that, I would never let her name pass my lips again either.'

Kate wanted the floor to open up and swallow her. Poor Luke… And she'd made things worse by opening her big mouth and reminding him of something it was obvious he would rather forget. Good grief…he hadn't even told Matteo his wife's name? Just referred to her as 'the cheating cow'?

And something else was trying to push its way into her consciousness.

The fact that Luke was single again?

No. She was too old and wise to allow any seed to grow in that long-ago abandoned space. She'd been romantically invisible back then. Why would that have changed?

What needed to change was the subject. Fast.

'How long were you in Milan?'

'Two years. And then I won a consultancy position six months ago. In Edinburgh.'

'No *way…*'

Luke blinked. 'What's so surprising about that? Did you think I was going to stay a registrar for ever?'

Kate shook her head. 'It's not that. I'm a consultant too. In Glasgow.'

Luke laughed. 'You mean we've been living fifty miles from each other and we had to travel halfway across Europe to catch up?'

'Not even fifty miles. Georgia and I live in

Brackenburn—halfway between Glasgow and Edinburgh. I work in the Eastern Infirmary in Glasgow and Georgie's a paramedic at a rescue base in Edinburgh.'

'Do you have helicopters?' Matteo asked Georgia.

'Yes. Two. I don't get to go up in them very often, though. Only when they're short of staff. You?'

'I've been a flight paramedic for eight years now. I love it…'

Kate and Luke weren't listening to the conversation between their partners. People around them were starting to move, which meant that the time for finding out exactly what tomorrow would bring was getting close.

But they were both sitting very still. So much had happened in the years since they'd last seen each other. Kate wanted to know more and she was saddened by more than a hint of bitterness in Luke's tone when he'd confirmed that his marriage was over. How could that have happened to one of the nicest people she had ever known?

Maybe something of what she was thinking was showing in her face.

'What about you, Katy?' Luke asked quietly. 'You happily married now? Got a couple of kids at home? That was the plan, wasn't it?'

Kate dropped her gaze. There was something a little shameful about admitting that she had failed to achieve her most important personal goals. She didn't say anything, simply shaking her head as she reached for her glass to finish her drink.

'We'd better get going,' Matteo said. 'It's time…'

Kate stood up, more than happy to leave this conversation behind for the moment.

But Luke stayed where he was for a moment, staring up at Kate.

'It was your birthday in March,' he said.

'It always is.' Kate grinned. 'Two weeks after yours, in fact.'

'Yeah…so we both turned thirty-five.'

Was he trying to rub in the fact that she was still single? That parenthood was probably still years away? That she might get into her forties and get past the point where it might be even possible?

She could feel defensive hackles begin to rise. Maybe, thanks to his own unfortunate experience, Luke had changed from being the nicest person in the world.

But he was grinning. And he didn't have to say a word for Kate to realise that he hadn't been trying to remind her that time was ticking on.

He was reminding her of something else. Something they'd agreed on after that legendary night of celebrating their final results as they'd graduated as fully fledged doctors. Something she hadn't thought about in at least five years.

Because it had become redundant the moment that Luke had got married.

Surely he didn't think it could be reinstated because he was single again?

No. Kate turned away with a dismissive shake of her head.

'The pact' was no longer in existence.

CHAPTER TWO

'I THINK WE'RE HERE.'

Kate looked at the two-storeyed village house they were parked in front of. The door was shut and there was nobody to be seen trying to flag down medical assistance. She had programmed the satellite navigation system with all the GPS coordinates of their daytime tasks herself, however, so she was confident that no mistakes had been made.

'We've got ten minutes. We'll knock on the door at precisely seven forty-five. You might want to turn off the light.' The portable flashing light on the top of the SUV was plugged into the car's cigarette lighter. 'We don't want to flatten the battery while we're on scene.'

'Roger that.' Georgia pulled the plug from the socket. She smiled at Kate but then her face scrunched into a grimace. 'First scenario. You nervous?'

'I wish we had some idea of what we're going to. The name doesn't give us much of a clue, does it? "Sweetheart"?'

'Maybe it's got something to do with sugar. A diabetic emergency, maybe?'

'Good thinking.'

'Or...' Georgia wiggled her eyebrows. 'Maybe it's a young couple who are madly in love and they were having morning sex in the shower and one of them has slipped over and hit their head on the side of the bath.'

Kate didn't want to think about people who were so crazy in love they couldn't keep their hands off each other. She'd never experienced that kind of love. Why was it that the balance always seemed to be tipped far too much in one direction? The people she fell in love with never felt the same way but if she was only mildly interested she could guarantee that the guy would fall head over heels for her and become suffocatingly attentive.

She checked her watch. 'Five minutes.'

'Do you think another team is still in there? Luke and Matteo, maybe?'

Kate didn't want to think about Luke, either. Not when thinking about the past could be a distraction. She had every intention of beating his team in this competition. It was her turn, after all. Payback for him getting better marks in finals.

He'd been so gracious about that, hadn't he? Toasting her with that excellent champagne he'd brought with him. The first bottle, that was. The second bottle had been a bad idea because it had culminated in concocting 'the pact' but the evening had been all about celebrating their graduation to start with. And each other's success.

'I owe it all to you, Katy. If you hadn't been my study buddy and I hadn't been trying so hard to keep up with your brilliance for the last few years, I'd probably have been at the bottom of the class.'

Not true, of course. Luke had one of the sharpest minds she'd ever had the pleasure of arguing with and, if she'd had the edge on remembering everything she learned, Luke had been better at the practical skills in those days. More confident, with surprisingly nimble fingers. It was no surprise that he had become a surgeon and Kate had no doubt that he was excelling in his field. Did those skills extend to an environment outside of an operating theatre? How much had Matteo taught him about front-line emergency procedures?

'Time?'

'Oh, help. It's seven forty-six.' How had *that* happened?

Both Kate and Georgia leapt from the vehicle, slamming the front doors to go around to the back and collect the well-stocked kits that Georgia's Edinburgh ambulance station had provided for them. She'd been distracted, Kate realised, by thinking about Luke.

It wasn't going to happen again.

'We're early.'

Luke grunted. Eight-fifteen was their start time for the scenario with the odd name of 'Sweet-

heart' but he'd been determined not to risk dis-
qualification by being late at any of the tasks
they'd been set for the day. Especially now, when
he had the added incentive of competing with
Kate.

Her turn to win?

He found himself smiling. Whatever the result,
this competition had just become a lot more fun.

The smile faded, however, as he looked around
them at the quiet street dotted with small, village
houses. 'Doesn't look like much.' A bit disap-
pointing, in fact. He'd expected to have something like a car versus pedestrian scenario for
the coordinates in the middle of this small town.
'You sure we're in the right place?'

'*Sì. Assolutamente.*' Matteo pointed through
the windscreen. 'That car parked over there is a
competitor. It's got the numbers. And a light on
the roof, like ours. And the flags are...'

'Scottish,' Luke murmured. There was only
one team representing Scotland here and he knew
who that was.

That smile was resurfacing. How astonishing

had it been to run into Kate here, of all places in the world?

And how good had it been to see her again?

It made him realise that he'd been lonely ever since he'd taken up his new position in Edinburgh. He'd missed his mate, Matteo, who'd been so good for him during his time in Milan as he'd licked his wounds after escaping the disaster that his marriage had been. Focusing so completely on work in Edinburgh had left no time to try and make new friends, which was probably why he'd taken up Matteo's invitation to join him for this competition.

And while it had been great to catch up with his mate, seeing Kate again was on a whole new level. They had history—heart-warming history—that made her like family.

He hadn't thought about that 'pact' for years.

Not until last night, that was, when Kate's avoidance of answering his query about whether she was married with kids yet had reminded him of how much time had passed. Plenty of time to have achieved the 'plan'.

The plan they'd discussed that night after graduation, over that really great bottle of champagne.

'Me? I'm going to start my stellar career and find the woman of my dreams to share the glory. What about you, Katy?'

'Oh... I'm going to have a brilliant career, too. And I'm going to find the man of my dreams and get married and have a couple of the world's most gorgeous children...'

And then they'd polished off that second bottle and things had become a whole lot more mushy. The 'plan' had morphed into the 'pact'.

'You're my best mate, Katy. I love you to bits.'

'Love you, too, mate.'

'Tell you what...'

'What?'

'If we haven't found those dream people by the time we're...oh...say, thirty-five...let's marry each other.'

'Why would you want to marry me?'

'I might be desperate by then.'

'Cheers, mate.'

'Oh, come on...it was a joke.'

'Your idea of getting married is a joke.'

'No... I'm serious. Let's make a pact. If we're both still single when we're thirty-five, we'll marry each other. Okay?'

She'd drained her glass of champagne, pushed her hair out of her eyes and given him a curiously intent stare. And then she'd done it. Agreed to the pact.

'Okay. You're on.'

'So it's a pact? Signed and sealed?'

'It's a pact. But now I need to go to sleep.'

Ancient memories but good ones.

Yes. It was extraordinarily good to see Kate again. Best of all, he had discovered that she lived close enough to his new home town that they would be able to see each other whenever they both had some free time.

Unless she had a boyfriend, of course. Thanks to Matteo's conversation with Georgia last night, he now knew that Kate wasn't married and that she was sharing a house with Georgia, but that didn't mean there wasn't someone else in the picture. Why wouldn't there be? Kate was gorgeous, with that impressive intelligence shining from those bright, blue eyes. And he liked that her hair was a bit longer these days. The blonde bob almost touched her shoulders and had a bit of a swing to it.

Not that it would be a problem if she had a significant other in her life. It could mean that Luke's circle of friends was about to expand, in fact. Maybe they could even double date. He and Matteo had had a lot of fun doing that in Milan. Nothing serious, mind you. Matteo might be dead keen to settle down and start a family of his own with the woman of his dreams but Luke had abandoned any such fairy-tale long ago. At about the same moment he'd learned that his marriage was a complete sham. As he'd remarked so bitterly to Kate, he had no intention of ever losing his head—or his heart—over a woman again.

Still…he wasn't getting any younger. It would be a shame to miss out completely and spend the rest of his life caring for other people's children…

* * *

The noise coming from the other side of the door was enough to make Kate and Georgia share a startled glance.

A party? At this time of the day?

Georgia pounded on the door. 'Ambulance,' she yelled.

There was no response, so she opened the door. They walked straight into a living room and there were at least half a dozen people, talking loudly enough to hear each other over the music. A bottle of vodka was being passed around and glasses clinked together. Nobody took the least bit of notice of the newcomers.

'Hello...' An earlier coin toss had decided that Kate was taking the lead role in this first scenario and she approached the nearest person. 'Did someone call for an ambulance?'

'Not me,' the young man replied. 'Hey...' He put his arm around a young woman. 'Let's dance...'

Kate blinked. This was nothing like she had expected. Where were the officials that would be judging their performance? Where was someone who looked remotely like a patient?

Georgia's eyes narrowed as she caught Kate's glance and she raised her voice loudly enough to be heard by everyone.

'*Oi...*'

The vodka carrier lowered the bottle. Heads turned in surprise.

'Someone called an ambulance,' Georgia said sternly. 'Who was it?'

'Oh...' There was a man sitting in the corner of the room, leaning on the wall. 'That was me. My girlfriend is upstairs. She's lying down because she has a bad stomach ache.'

'Anything else we should know?'

'No. I don't think so.' The man raised a glass as he smiled at them. 'Oh, she is pregnant. Is that important?'

Turning swiftly, they raced up a narrow set of stairs to find themselves in a bedroom and here it was. The scenario...

Two judges with clipboards were standing by. A young woman was sitting on a bed and she was holding a manikin of a newborn infant wrapped in a T-shirt.

'Check mum and get her history,' Kate told Georgia. 'I'll check the baby.'

The young mother didn't want to let go of her baby.

'How long ago was the baby born?'

'Only a minute…maybe two…'

'Have you heard it cry?'

'No. *No*… Please don't take my baby away…'

'It's okay,' Georgia told her. 'We just want to help you. Kate's a baby doctor.'

Kate moved the folds of the T-shirt to reveal the baby's face. The cord was wrapped tightly around the baby's neck.

'The baby is blue,' one of the judges said.

Kate scooped the manikin from the patient's arms. She turned to find that Georgia had stopped her examination of the mother for the moment. She'd laid a towel on the floor and had the kit opened, with the paediatric resuscitation gear that Kate would need within easy reach. A suction bulb, a tiny bag mask unit and tubes in case intubation was necessary.

'No significant haemorrhage from the mother,' Georgia told her. 'And she has a radial pulse.'

Kate nodded approvingly. 'Thanks.' If the mother had a radial pulse it indicated that her blood pressure was adequate and that meant they could both focus on saving the life of this baby.

She laid the baby on the towel and positioned its head to ensure the airway was clear.

'Can I feel a pulse?' Kate asked swiftly, her fingers now on the baby's neck.

'The pulse is thirty,' the judge said.

'Can I see or feel any movements of respiration?' Kate already knew what the answer was likely to be. This infant hadn't cried and its colour meant that it was receiving no more oxygen than the umbilical cord was hopefully still providing.

'The baby is not breathing,' the judge confirmed.

Kate gave five puffs of oxygen through the bag mask unit and then started CPR, which was needed even though there was a pulse to be felt. The heart rate was too slow and the baby wasn't breathing on its own yet.

She handed the bag mask to Georgia, who had positioned herself at the baby's head.

'Three to one?'

Georgia nodded. With only two fingers on the baby's chest, Kate kept her compressions gentle but swift. After every three compressions, she paused for a moment to allow Georgia to administer a puff of air. At the same time, she kept an eye on the mother, reassuring her that they were doing all they could and watching for any signs of a post-partum haemorrhage that they would need to manage.

Every thirty seconds, she checked what the baby's heart rate was. It crept up to forty and then sixty.

'The heart rate is now over eighty,' the judge informed them after a few minutes.

'Colour?'

'Getting pink.'

'Breathing?'

'Yes, she's breathing. She's crying now.' The judge was smiling. 'Well done.'

Kate put the baby back into its mother's arms and wrapped them both warmly. 'Keep her against your skin,' she said.

'Is she going to be all right?'

'She's going to be fine.' Kate smiled. 'Congratulations. You have a beautiful baby daughter.'

The young woman was a very good actor. Kate could swear she had tears of relief in her eyes as she thanked her rescuers and cuddled her newborn. The whole scenario had felt so real that Kate found she was having an emotional response of her own. One that she had had many times in her career—the sheer wonder of a new life being brought into the world and...

And envy of the mother who got to hold it and know it was her own?

Good grief. The baby was plastic and the whole scenario, however brilliantly acted, was not real. While this competition set out to test and even improve the skills of the participants, it was nothing more than a game. Kate needed to step back and not become so involved with the stories or she would be too exhausted to be a good partner for Georgia by the time the night tasks came along.

'That was awesome,' Georgia said, as soon as they shut the front door behind them again. '*You* were awesome. I think we smashed that one.'

'We certainly saved the baby. And the judges looked happy.' Kate checked her watch and then opened the back hatch of the car. 'We've only got ten minutes to locate our next task. We'd better get a move on.'

But Georgia had paused. She was waving. 'Look—there's Matteo and Luke in that car. They must be next.'

'I wonder how long it'll take before they figure out their patient isn't downstairs.' Kate felt a sudden urge to help Luke out. To give him a clue…

'It's no wonder it's against the rules to talk about the scenarios until it's all over.' Georgia slung her kit into the back. 'And I got the feeling that Matteo is as much a stickler for the rules as you are, Kate. You two would get on very well.'

'I'm not here on a man hunt. What's the matter? Don't you like him?'

Georgia shrugged. 'He's cute but there are a lot of fish in this particular sea and today is not the day to be casting my net.'

Kate snorted. She knew Georgia quite well enough to know that she wasn't the least bit serious about finding a casual sexual partner just for fun. This was just bravado, that was all. Was she trying to prove to the world that she was over the last disaster and more than ready to move on?

Pausing for a moment, before climbing into the driver's seat, Kate turned her head to look at the car parked a little further up the road. She lifted her hand in greeting and, by the instant response as he raised his, she knew that Luke had been watching her.

A weird frisson of something she couldn't identify rippled through her belly. Was it a little disturbing to have someone from her past suddenly appear in her life like this? As if Luke was some kind of ghost?

Or was it just nice to have reconnected with an old and very dear friend?

Yeah…that had to be it. Because the feeling was too pleasant to be a warning.

'Look…they're coming out of the house.'

Luke found himself hunkering down in his seat a little. It was pure coincidence that they were the next team for this particular scenario but, oddly, it felt like he was pushing himself back into Kate's life or something. Stalking her, even? Was she as pleased to see him as he'd been to see her?

Maybe not. It had been Georgia who'd spotted them and waved. Kate had seemed intent on putting her gear back into the car and checking her watch. Of course she would be making sure she was going to be on time for the next task—that was so like Kate. Responsible and reliable. And she was taking this contest seriously, as she did everything she became involved with.

It looked as though she was going to get in the car and simply drive off, but then she paused and looked straight at him and there was a smile to go with her wave.

Luke let out a breath he hadn't realised he'd been holding as he raised his hand in response. A sigh of something like relief as something clicked back into place. The connection of their friendship, perhaps, where he didn't have to worry about how his actions might be interpreted. A place he could relax in and simply be himself.

'Be nice to have an idea of what we're heading into,' he said. 'They weren't giving away any clues, were they?'

'And neither should they,' Matteo said sternly. 'That would be dishonest.'

'Not exactly.' Matteo liked to have his English improved. 'Dishonesty is when you fail to tell the truth. Breaking the rules of the competition to give someone else an advantage would be dishonourable rather than dishonest.'

'Hmm...' Matteo absorbed the correction. 'They are both unacceptable.'

'Too right they are,' Luke agreed.

The first scenario was initially confusing but,

as soon as they discovered that the party was a
red herring, the two men worked well on their
paediatric resuscitation. In the next task, they
found a man who'd summoned an ambulance
because of sudden back pain and nausea. Diag-
nosing a case of kidney stones was easy but there
was a twist in the case because the man had an
anaphylactic allergic reaction to the morphine
they administered for pain relief.

The twist was unexpected but Matteo spotted the first symptoms within seconds and they
both reacted swiftly, attaching a bag of fluids to
the IV line already in place and drawing up and
administering drugs to counteract the reaction.
Then they had to answer questions from one of
the judges about which of the available hospitals
they would be transferring their patient to.

'Hospital A,' Luke told them. 'They have an
internal medicine department and an intensive
care unit and they are the closest.'

'And what is the most important information
to pass on about your patient?'

'That he has a previously undiscovered allergy

to morphine. We will write it on his notes and make sure the information is received by everyone we speak to. We will also advise the patient that it would be a good idea to wear a medic alert bracelet from now on.'

'That was good.' Matteo slapped Luke on the back as they left the house. 'I might not have thought of recommending the bracelet.'

'I was too slow to spot the change in our patient's condition. Well done, you.'

Matteo grinned at him. 'We make a good team.'

'We've got a break now, haven't we? About an hour?'

'We should use it to do the driving test.'

'Okay.' The driving test was something they could do at any point of the day. A gravelled area beside the river that ran through this village had been cordoned off. A line of orange road cones marked the test area. They could see an ambulance completing the test as they arrived, clouds of dust billowing as it snaked around the cones at high speed and then came to a sudden halt between the cones marking the end of the course.

Another car was waiting for its turn.

The car with the Scottish flags.

'Cute.' Matteo grinned. 'I didn't notice that before.'

Luke raised his eyebrows. 'You mean Georgia? Or Kate?' He wasn't sure he liked the idea of Matteo being attracted to Kate. Then he shook the reaction off. Why not? Matteo was a great guy and the best friend he'd had since Kate had vanished from his life. He'd make some lucky woman an ideal husband and father for her children and, if Kate felt the same way, he should do his best to make it happen.

But Matteo was laughing. 'Oh, the girls are both cute but that wasn't what I was looking at. Have you seen what is tied to the front of their car?'

No. Because Luke had been looking at Kate who was standing beside the car, talking to Georgia who was in the driver's seat. He glanced at the stuffed toy bear that was wearing a kilt and holding a set of bagpipes.

Matteo rolled down his window and pointed to the toy. 'He is going to get dirty, I think.'

'All part of the fun,' Georgia called back. 'Which one of you is going to do the driving? You're only allowed one person in the vehicle.'

Georgia was clearly the one doing the test for their team. Luke glanced at Matteo and unclipped his seat belt.

'You do it,' he said. 'You've got far more experience with emergency driving skills than I have. I'll wait with Kate.'

'Cool.' Matteo was already focussed on what Georgia was doing to see what his turn would involve.

Luke walked over to where Kate was standing, well away from where the dust clouds would drift.

'How's it all going?' he asked.

'Great.' Kate's expression was animated and she opened her mouth again as if she couldn't wait to tell him about something but then it snapped shut and the excitement faded into disappointment. 'But we can't talk about it yet.'

'No.' It was a moment longer before Luke turned away from watching her face. Did she have any idea how much of what she was thinking was revealed in how quickly her expressions could change? He'd forgotten that about conversations with Kate. Forgotten how entertaining it was.

They both watched Georgia as she careened through the serpentine, knocking over a couple of cones.

'She's a bit wild.'

'Enthusiastic,' Kate conceded. 'But she'll get another go. The team before us had three goes.'

So they had a few minutes, then. And nothing to talk about?

'Where did you say that you're working in Glasgow? At the Western?'

'No. The Eastern. We're a specialised maternity and paediatric hospital. Best PICU in Scotland.'

Luke nodded. 'Yes...some of our surgical cases have been transferred there. Are you based in PICU?'

'No. I'm on the wards as a senior paediatric registrar. I do the occasional shift in Emergency as well.'

'Are you happy?'

Kate's eyes widened. 'With the job? Of course. I've always loved working with kids.'

Luke wanted to know what that flicker in her eyes suggested. That she wasn't happy with her life away from work?

'I remember,' was all he said. 'You had a rapport with small people right from the start. How come you haven't got some of your own now? You never said last night...'

'Huh? Some of my own what?'

'Kids.'

'No.' Kate's gaze slid away from his to watch Georgia's second attempt at the course. 'I will, though. One day. It's certainly still part of the grand plan.'

There was a wistful note in her voice. A flick of a glance that made him wonder if she was hearing the echoes of that champagne-doused conversation. Remembering his plan to have a stellar career and find the woman of his dreams to share the glory with?

His breath came out in a soft snort. Ah, well… he was well on the way to the career he'd dreamed of, at least. He flicked a glance back at Kate.

'So you've got a potential father lined up?'

Kate shaded her eyes against the sun. 'That's better, Georgia, but you're too slow now…'

'A partner?' Luke persisted. 'A boyfriend? Any kind of significant other?'

Kate sighed, sounding a little exasperated. 'No.'

Luke was silent for a moment, digesting the information, as Georgia circled back to where the officials were standing. They seemed to be having a discussion about whether she would have another attempt.

So Kate was single.

This was good, he decided. It meant that there were no barriers to them spending some time together and he didn't have to find someone so that they could double date.

This was more than good. It was excellent.

'And you're thirty-five...' Oh, help. Had he said that aloud?

Judging by Kate's dismissive snort, she had heard the impulsive statement.

'I can't believe you even remember that, given how drunk you were at the time.'

Kate had been just as enthusiastic about opening that second bottle of champagne. And *she* obviously remembered the pact...

'Anyway, it's null and void now. You got married.'

'Hey... I made a mistake.' Luke kept his tone light. 'You don't need to rub my nose in it.'

'Sorry.' Kate offered him a smile. 'Good thing you didn't have kids, I guess. Or did you?'

'No. Thank goodness. It was a clean—and complete—breakup.'

There was a moment's silence. Georgia was lining up to have what would probably be her last attempt at the driving test. Matteo was leaning out of his window, watching carefully.

Kate was also watching carefully but Luke couldn't resist the opportunity to tease her a little.

'The pact didn't have any sub-clauses that I remember,' he said. 'Didn't we solemnly declare that if we were both still single when we were thirty five, we would marry each other?'

The glance Kate gave him over her shoulder was dismissive. 'Thanks, but I intend to give it a bit more time. I haven't given up on true love yet. My soul mate is out there somewhere—I just haven't found him yet.'

Luke had to groan. 'You don't really believe in that, do you? Finding 'the one'?'

He could see her shoulders stiffen. And her voice was cool. 'Maybe I want what you and Nadia had.'

'*No.*' The word came out with unexpected vehemence. 'You don't.'

'It was great when it started, though, wasn't it? I'd never seen you so happy.'

There was that wistful note again and Luke's brain broke the rules and dredged up a memory of what it had been like to be so in love. How magic it had been. He shut down the memory instantly. He didn't need that kind of magic in

his life now because that was all it was. A spell.
One that could be reversed with no more than a
click of someone's fingers to leave devastation
in its wake.

Kate broke the silence. Maybe she realised
she'd stirred up something unpleasant for him
because her tone was gentle.

'You just found it with the wrong person,' she
said.

'And you think you can find the right one?'

'I hope so.'

'How will you know?' Luke was genuinely cu-
rious.

'I don't know exactly,' Kate admitted. 'I guess
I'll have to trust my instincts.'

'Good luck with that.' Luke was more than
happy to leave this conversation. He was relieved
to see that Georgia was driving back towards
them, passing Matteo who went to take his position at the start. 'I really hope you'll find him,'
he added. 'And that you'll live happily ever after.'

Kate smiled at him. 'So you agree that the pact
is null and void, then?'

Luke shrugged. 'I'm over the whole marriage thing, anyway. Been there, got the T-shirt. Friendship's better.' He smiled back at Kate. 'Seems to last a lot longer, too.'

He could see sympathy in Kate's eyes. And something more. Something warm.

'You're right. True friendship is the most important thing in the world.' Her breath came out in a sigh as she smiled again. 'It's really good to see you again, Luke.'

'Likewise. We'll have to make sure we don't lose touch when we get back home. I'm still a fish out of water in Scotland. I haven't had time to meet anybody, apart from the people I work with, yet. I haven't been anywhere or seen anything, either.'

'I haven't done much sightseeing myself,' Kate told him, as Georgia joined them. 'I'm sure there are some great places to go in Scotland.'

'Are you kidding?' Georgia sounded offended. 'It's the most beautiful country in the world. We've got the most gorgeous lakes and forests and more castles than could ever wish for.' She grinned. 'The weather can be a bit grey and wet, of course, but it's summer now. You'll get at least three days of sunshine.'

'It's a plan, then,' Kate said. 'The first day we both have off, we'll go and find something to see.'

'Even if it's not one of the three sunny days?'

Kate laughed. 'I don't mind rain. You get to find a lovely old pub with a roaring open fire and have a long lunch.'

The sun was shining on them right now and Luke was feeling good. That unpleasant reminder of failure in his personal life was well buried again and the future was suddenly looking a lot brighter.

He had the promise of expanding his horizons. Of a new country to explore and company that he knew would make it a lot more fun. Waving Kate and Georgia off as they headed for their next task, he found himself smiling.

He was even hoping that it would rain on that day off. He was looking forward to one of those long lunches.

CHAPTER THREE

THE STEW AND potato dumplings on offer for lunch were rapidly becoming unappetisingly familiar.

Not that Georgia was bothered.

'I'm starving,' she told Kate as they handed over their vouchers and found a place to sit in the dining area. 'I feel like I've been on a full shift already and we're only a third of our way through the competition. At least we get a break after this. I'm going to try and catch a nap.'

Kate wasn't that bothered either. She was barely tasting her food, in fact.

After they'd eaten, they wandered outside and found a grassy patch to lie on under a shady tree. Georgia promptly closed her eyes and gave every appearance of having fallen asleep but Kate found herself staring up at the play of light on leaves dancing in a soft breeze.

The pact had been dismissed.

It had been a relief not to have to argue any more about any lingering validity to that vow they'd made but, oddly, there was a feeling curiously like disappointment in the wake of that relief.

Why?

She'd made such a determined effort to get past that crush when she'd first met Luke. To get over the heartbreak of watching him get attracted to other women. She'd only ever been one of his close circle of friends and, in the end, she'd embraced that position in his life because it was a whole lot better than not having him in *her* life.

He'd never seen her as anything more than a friend, she knew that for sure. Such a good friend that those around them at medical school had commented more than once that they were perfect for each other and that they should make it official, but both Kate and Luke had laughed off the suggestions. Because Kate would never forget the first time it had happened—the look of shock in Luke's eyes as they'd caught each other's gazes. The embarrassment that the idea of having sex with a friend had generated.

It had been the final push to give up any remnants of that crush and she'd done it so successfully that the next time someone said something, she'd actually felt that same embarrassment herself.

But the pact had been a product of how much they'd cared about each other and, looking back now, Kate remembered that it had been almost an insurance policy and actually a comfort on more than one occasion when a relationship had hit the wall.

Only until Luke had married Nadia, of course. After that, she'd had to cope without the comfort of reminding herself that *someone* would still want her when she'd been on the shelf so long that her use-by date had expired.

And now she *was* that age and it was only the pact that had expired. Despite both Luke and Georgia's disenchantment with the whole busi-

ness, she really did believe in love. In finding
her soul mate. Someone that she would fall totally in love with and who would feel the same
way about her. She knew what that felt like because she'd come close enough to touch it in the
early stages of a past romance or two and she'd
recognised the moment that the elusive goal had
slipped from her fingers. The moment when it
had become obvious that they weren't right for
each other. The moment when the flicker had
sputtered and died…

There was no such thing as a use-by date, she
told herself. She had all the time in the world. She
just had to silence that malevolent little voice in
the back of her head that was not in agreement.
The one that whispered in a taunting tone.

*You know there's a use-by date on some dreams,
Kate. Just how long do you think you've got to
keep looking? Until you're forty-five and too old
to hope for that baby to hold in your arms?*

Was that what the disappointment was about?
That, subconsciously, she had welcomed the idea
that the insurance policy had been reinstated

and that, even if she didn't find the love of her life, she could still have the family she'd always dreamed of?

How ridiculous.

Yes, she loved Luke but it was still only a friendship. She'd worked hard to make that a reality for both of them and, honestly, she'd been barely more than a teenager when she'd hoped for something more. She was grown up now and so was Luke. They were different people in many ways.

And the idea of having sex with him was still too embarrassing to even think about. It would be as bad as confessing the crush he'd been so oblivious to.

This was more like it.

The scene that Luke and Matteo entered that afternoon as their ninth task was exactly the kind of scenario that they'd expected from such a famous, international competition.

It was set in a huge park and it was a multicasualty incident of a mini-bus crash. As the two men approached the cordoned-off area that had many spectators surrounding it, they took in the bus crumpled against a huge tree and a person lying motionless nearby. They could see people wandering aimlessly around, including a woman holding a blood-stained cloth to her head, and they could hear cries coming from inside the bus.

'Wow...'

Not only must it have been a mammoth undertaking to set this scenario up, Luke could see that it had been duplicated on the other side of the park so that more than one team at a time could compete.

Matteo was leading this scene.

'I think this is a triage exercise,' he told Luke, quietly. 'We don't stop to treat anything unless it's immediately life-threatening.' He pulled some brightly coloured labels from the kit as he raised his voice. 'Anyone who can walk, please come here.'

People began moving. A man climbed out of the bus. They all looked visibly shaken and some had minor injuries like scrapes and bruises. The man who had come out of the bus was holding his arm as if it hurt to move it.

'The driver,' one of them said. 'He's bad…'

'There's a woman still on the bus…' another person told them. 'She has a little boy…'

'Stay here,' Luke ordered the small group. 'We'll be back.'

Matteo was already beside the man lying on the ground. Their first patient was conscious and Luke could hear him as he got closer.

'It hurts,' he groaned. 'It hurts so much…'

He could talk, so his airway wasn't a problem. There was no obvious haemorrhage that needed to be stopped but he was clearly in severe pain, possibly with internal injuries, so he was tagged with a green label as status two—needing urgent treatment but no immediate life-saving measures.

'We'll be right back,' Luke promised. 'As soon as we check to see who else needs help.'

The woman with the head injury was confused and trying to wander away from the scene and she was rubbing at her neck as if it hurt. Matteo put the rubber band of another green label around her wrist and then called to one of the men in the uninjured group and gave him the task of looking after her.

'Get her to sit down and try to keep her head still so she doesn't move her neck. Don't let her go anywhere. We'll be back.'

Then they climbed into the bus. The driver was slumped over the steering wheel. A judge was seated near the front of the bus.

Luke lifted the man's head to open his airway. He felt for a carotid pulse in the man's neck.

'There is no pulse,' the judge told him.

Luke and Matteo shared a glance. Had the bus crashed because the driver had had a cardiac arrest? This was not the time to start a resuscitation that would take all their attention and stop them treating people that were more likely to be saved. This patient got a white label to indicate that he was deceased—a status zero.

There was a woman towards the back of the bus who had a small boy cuddled beside her. He looked to be about six years old and was taking his acting job very seriously.

'You have to help my mother,' he told his rescuers. 'She keeps going to sleep.'

'We will,' Luke promised. 'Are *you* hurt anywhere?'

Matteo was leaning over the back of the seat, talking to the woman.

'My leg is trapped,' she whispered. 'I can't get out. Help me…'

'We will,' he promised.

'I have a sore foot, too,' the boy told Luke.

'My leg hurts so much,' the woman groaned. 'Please…help me…'

Matteo was taking her pulse.

'The heart rate is one hundred and twenty,' the judge told him.

'Colour?'

'As you see her. She's very pale and sweaty.'

Matteo leaned further over the seat. 'I see blood on the floor. Is this a significant loss?'

'Yes.'

'Take the boy out to the others,' Matteo directed Luke. 'I need to control the bleeding.'

Luke scooped the boy into his arms and he obligingly wrapped his arms around Luke's neck.

'Do a secondary survey on the green-tag people,' Matteo added. 'And decide which hospital we need to transport them to. Get a cervical collar on the woman with the sore neck.' He already had a dressing in his hand and was applying pressure to the wound on the woman's leg but he was looking at the judge now. 'I need radio contact with the communication centre. Is there a helicopter available?'

Luke carried the little boy to the door and carefully down the steps.

'What's your name?' he asked.

'Ivan.'

'Are you having fun today, Ivan?'

'Yes.' The child's grin was impish and Luke had to smile back.

'Me, too,' he confessed.

Kate hadn't expected to have to walk so far carrying her heavy pack but this scenario was well off the road, in a park setting. As they came out of the woodland path, she could see what they were heading for and it took her breath away.

'Oh, my God…a *bus* crash?'

'It'll be a triage exercise,' Georgia told her. 'We'll have to check everybody and decide who needs the most urgent treatment. We'll only have to do something if it's immediately life-threatening, like a compromised airway or severe bleeding. They'll want us to decide what backup we need and which hospitals we are going to send patients to. And whether we call for air rescue backup.'

'Okay…' Georgia was focused on the area they were heading towards but Kate turned her head for a moment. Through the trees on one side, she could see that the scene had been duplicated. A team was already working there and she knew she shouldn't be trying to see what was going on but that single glance had given her a picture that froze in her head.

For a moment, all she got was the impression of a tall man wearing a high-vis vest and a helmet. A very good-looking man. It was a shock, in the next moment, to realise that it was Luke. She'd never seen him in a uniform like this before—was that what had made him look so different for a heartbeat?

He was walking away from the bus and he had a small boy in his arms. The child had his arms wrapped around Luke's neck but he didn't look as if he was supposed to be badly injured. He was smiling, in fact. And Luke was smiling back at him as if they were sharing a joke.

And, just for another instant, before she could bury the image and focus on what she knew was going to be a full-on task, Kate found her own lips curving into a smile. Something warm blossomed somewhere in her chest. Or maybe in her belly. The kind of melting sensation that she had sometimes when she saw the fathers of some of her tiny patients being so gentle and caring with their precious children.

Luke had sounded more than relieved when he'd confirmed that he and Nadia hadn't had a baby but surely he wanted to be a father one day?

He'd be the *best* father... Kind and funny and clever and so very, very caring...

Had Nadia had any idea of what she'd thrown away?

How could she have been so *stupid*?

Mist clung to the mountains and shrouded the trees as dawn broke the next day and the two friends made their way home after the series of night tasks.

They'd dealt with a young man having an acute stroke as a side effect of an incorrect drug dosage for hypertension, followed by a cardiac-arrest scenario in someone's house where the manikin available for CPR was linked to a computer that gave a printout of how effective their compressions and ventilation efforts had been. As if that hadn't been enough, they'd finished up with a mass shooting incident at a teenager's birthday party where they seemed to be working with teams of police officers who were having a scene management competition of their own.

'I haven't been this tired since those night shifts

in my first hospital job when I'd already worked the day and had to keep going through the next day.'

'I know.' Georgia was looking pale with fatigue herself. 'Let's get some breakfast and then we'll have a few hours to sleep before the debrief.'

'I'm too tired to feel hungry.'

'Me, too. Let's just go to bed.'

The car door felt ridiculously heavy as Kate pushed it open when they'd parked near the accommodation block. Climbing the stairs felt like a mountain challenge and even having a shower was going to require too much effort. Kate lay down on the single bed opposite Georgia's and let her breath out in a sigh that was close to a groan.

Her body was telling her that this had been the craziest idea ever.

Her heart had something else to say, however. She was very glad that she had come. Not only had it been an experience that had deepened her friendship with Georgia and one that she would remember for the rest of her life, it felt like its effects could quite possibly change her world for the better in the near future.

That image of Luke with the little boy in his arms floated back into her mind and she fell asleep with a smile on her face.

Maybe that was why Kate felt so much better when their alarm went off four hours later.

And why she put a little extra effort into getting ready for the debrief session, where the judges were going to go over every scenario and tell them how they would have gained the highest scores. A lot of competitors would probably give the session a miss in favour of some more sleep before the social events of the prize-giving, convoy drive and the big party tonight but Kate knew that Luke would be going. He'd want to know exactly how well he'd done and—if he'd missed an expected diagnosis or intervention along the way—Kate could be quite sure that he'd be taking some notes so that it would never happen again.

When she entered the large room to see him sitting near the back with a notebook already open on his lap, she hid her smile.

He hadn't changed a bit, had he?

Except he did look older. Maybe because he had to be as tired as she was. Or maybe it was a sense of maturity that only came with age and the accrued wisdom of bitter experience.

He'd been through some tough times, hadn't he?

He glanced up, as if he was suddenly aware of the sympathy coming in his direction. His face was blank until he focussed on Kate and then his expression changed instantly. He wasn't smiling but the deepening of the crinkles around his eyes created enough warmth for Kate to feel it all the way down to her toes.

The same kind of warmth she'd felt when she'd seen him with that small child in his arms yesterday.

She slipped into the seat beside him.

'Where's Matteo?'

'Sleeping. I told him I'd take notes and tell him what we did wrong over lunch.'

Kate laughed. 'He and Georgia have a lot in common. She just groaned and rolled over when our alarm went off.'

'We might regret getting up when we fall asleep at the party tonight.'

Kate was still smiling as she held his gaze for a moment longer. Not likely. She and Luke had a lot in common, too, and one thing they'd always shared was a determination to learn from every experience and use that knowledge to make them better at the profession they both had a passion for.

Overall, it seemed like she and Georgia had done well in all the scenarios. Luke was looking pleased with his team's performance, too.

'Did you activate the air rescue service for the guy with internal injuries at the bus crash?'

'Yes. Did you?'

'Yes. But we missed the clue that that teacher at the school had vodka in her juice bottle.'

'The hypoglycaemic emergency?' Luke grinned. 'I would have needed vodka too, I reckon, with that mob of naughty children. We had one climbing out of the window while we were trying to get a blood glucose and get an IV line in the patient.'

'Georgia had them under control in no time flat. And she got the school caretaker to take them away before we started any treatment.' Kate's spirits lifted. Control of that disruption had been one of the scoring points in that scenario. Maybe they'd done better than the other teams and would place at the prize-giving.

'You looking forward to the convoy? Did you hear the rumour that the local vet has to go around all the villages and give the horses a sedative so they don't freak out with the noise of all the sirens?'

'Really?' Kate frowned. 'And the owners are happy about that?'

'I guess so. They'll be out with everyone else, I reckon, watching us all drive by. It's a big event around here. Hey... Matteo suggested that you girls might like to come with us in our car. That way you can enjoy the view without having to drive.'

'I'll check with Georgia but it sounds like fun. She'll want to fly the Scottish flag, though.'

'That's fine by me. I'm kind of Scottish myself now.'

'That's right—you are…' The reminder that she and Luke were practically going to be neighbours as soon as they got home added to Kate's rising spirits. Any remaining fatigue was evaporating. The remaining time at this competition held the promise of being great fun.

It was a promise that delivered a lot more than Kate had anticipated. Georgia was more than happy to be a passenger in a shared vehicle and the two teams joined the others gathering in the town square for the prize-giving ceremony. It was a generous and good-natured crowd and the congratulatory cheers got louder as each award was bestowed. There were prizes for the doctor-only teams, the medical students, and the paramedics. She and Georgia shared a delighted glance when the team from New Zealand came second in their category.

'Special category P2,' the master of ceremonies announced eventually. 'One physician plus a maximum of two paramedics.'

Kate held her breath. She knew there'd been other teams in this category that had a doctor and two paramedics. Surely they would have done better than teams like hers and Luke's where there was only one paramedic?

'And the winner is...'

Kate turned her head to find Luke looking at her instead of the master of ceremonies.

'*Scotland...*'

Kate's jaw dropped and her head jerked sideways as Georgia let out a squeal of delight. The two women threw their arms around each other for a brief, fierce hug before making their way to the stage to receive their trophy. She looked back for a moment, however, before they began threading their way through the clapping crowd.

Yes... Matteo might be looking a bit disappointed but there was genuine delight written all over Luke's face.

He was proud of her.

'Champagne's on us tonight,' he called after

her. His grin stretched. 'Just like the old days, isn't it?'

Kate nodded, knowing her grin was just as wide as his.

She looked for him again as she stood on the stage beside Georgia, holding one side of the plaque commemorating their success, as a photo was taken.

He was wrong, she decided as her heart skipped a beat when her gaze had found what she'd been searching for.

It wasn't like the old days at all.

There was something very different now.

Something new.

Rather exciting, even?

She knew what it was, too.

She didn't feel invisible any more.

'Pull your head in, Kate!'

Matteo was slowing their vehicle, tooting the horn in greeting as they got closer to another group of people standing by the roadside, excited children in front of the adults with their hands held out expectantly.

'But they can't reach…' Kate had to shout over the noise. They were nose-to-tail in a procession of dozens of emergency vehicles that all had their sirens blaring and their warning lights flashing. She was leaning right out of the window, her hands full of the small gifts they'd obviously stocked up on before leaving Scotland. Thistle badges, key rings with kilted Highlanders holding bagpipes, bars of Highland toffee and boiled sweets in the colours of the Scottish flag.

Georgia was hanging onto Kate's shirt, trying to make sure she didn't actually fall out of the car as Matteo accelerated again, but she was laughing. The excitement of this whole experience had clearly gone to her head as well. Luke swivelled in the front seat in time to see Kate sit down again with a thump. She was laughing, too.

'Your turn next, Georgie. Look—there's lots of people on your side of the road coming up. Give some stuff to Luke.'

'I'm not about to lean out and risk getting my

head bumped.' But Luke had to grin. 'I can't believe I'm seeing you break the rules like this, Kate.'

'Yeah...' Georgia elbowed her friend. 'You heard them. No alcohol, no speeding and no leaning out of vehicles.'

Kate just pushed wind-blown hair out of her eyes and beamed back at them.

'But it's fun,' she said.

Luke had to admit that this was, indeed, great fun. But he wasn't sure what he was enjoying more. This extraordinary convoy or seeing Kate let her hair down and embrace the atmosphere so enthusiastically?

Maybe he was still feeling happy for her that she'd won the trophy. Or simply because they'd reconnected and there was no reason that Kate couldn't continue to be part of his life after this event was over. There wasn't even the obstacle of her having a boyfriend, which had been a huge— and, he had to admit, not an unpleasant surprise.

Perhaps friendship lacked the kind of excitement that falling in love might provide but it was even better. Because it was safer. He could relax with Kate and simply be himself with no danger of losing his head—or his heart. He'd been reminded of what it had been like to fall in love when Kate had been starry-eyed over what it had been like for him and Nadia in the beginning, but he was older and wiser now. As he'd told her, he'd been there and got the T-shirt.

Only that didn't really sum it up, did it?

You could throw away a T-shirt and its pithy message, like 'Marriage Sucks', but you couldn't get rid of the message he'd been left with. The words might be invisible but they'd been branded into his skin as a permanent reminder. Perhaps it was just as well that Kate had dismissed any idea that their 'pact' might still be valid.

Georgia was behaving just as badly as her best friend, leaning out of her window to distribute their small gifts as the children ran alongside the car, but Luke threw his into the waiting hands and returned the delighted grins when a catch was successful. In the wing mirror, he could see them scrambling to collect items that had landed on the grassy verge and then jumping to their feet as they awaited the vehicles still to pass.

The smile never left his face. He loved kids. The highlight of all the scenarios in this competition for him had been when he'd shared that moment with Ivan—the little boy who had been one of the actors in the bus-crash scenario. That moment of connection, when they'd both admitted their secret enjoyment of what was supposed to be a serious matter, had been priceless.

The pang that made his smile finally fade came from nowhere. How much stronger would a connection like that be if it was with a child of your own? He might have given up on the fairy-tale of marrying the love of your life that Kate still believed in but he wasn't ready to give up on the idea of having a family of his own. Lots of people settled for something far less than a passionate love story to achieve that, didn't they? They found someone they could respect and care about deeply and they learned to build a life together that was strong enough to protect the children they chose to bring into the world.

A glance into the rear-view mirror gave him a glimpse of Kate's profile, her blonde hair streaming back from her face as she tilted her head out of the window to see what lay ahead. Her cheeks were flushed and her eyes as bright as that happy smile.

Wow…

How come he'd never noticed how gorgeous she was in the old days?

She'd been right there all the time but she'd just been one of the gang. Just another great mate.

Shifting his gaze to the windscreen, Luke could see another bunch of children waiting with their parents. A father had a small child on his shoulders and a mother had a well-wrapped baby in her arms.

Families…

He couldn't help another glance in the rear-view mirror.

From this new, slightly more considered point of view, the concept of that pact he and Kate had made wasn't really so silly after all.

* * *

The final gathering of competitors, team members, families and officials was the perfect end to a time that Kate was never going to forget.

The combination of an extended period of such intense competition, fatigue and—for some—the pride of achievement made for a party atmosphere like nothing she had ever encountered before. It began with that astonishing convoy when Kate hadn't hesitated to break the rules and it just kept going.

There was champagne to be found and delicious barbecued food and so many people who now had a lot in common and wanted to enjoy the company of new friends or renew and deepen friendships that had been made in previous years because this event was an annual highlight for the majority of the participants.

'So who thinks they'll do this again?' Luke and Matteo were sitting at an outside picnic table, opposite Kate and Georgia. They were hemmed in by people from New Zealand, Croatia and Germany, and there seemed to be some friendly rivalry going on as to which team could provide the most in the way of beverages.

'Me.' Georgia and Matteo spoke at the same time and then grinned at each other and raised their glasses in a toast.

'I'd love to,' Dave the New Zealander said. 'Shame it's such a long way to come, which makes it horrendously expensive.' He winked at Georgia. 'I'll just have to start saving up, won't I?'

'We come every year,' a Croatian paramedic put in. 'And it gets better every time.'

Luke was looking at Kate, his eyebrows raised.

'Ask me next week…' she smiled '…when I've had enough sleep to be able to think straight.'

Luke leaned closer. 'We could do it together,' he suggested. 'As a doctor team.'

'Hey…' Georgia was scowling. 'You're not stealing my doctor partner.' She hooked her arm over Kate's shoulders. 'If anyone's going to do it again with Katy, it'll be *me*…'

But Kate smiled at Luke. She liked that he could see them being partners. And she liked that he was already thinking of a future that included her.

'I'm not sure that I'd want to do it again,' she said, 'but I'm very, very glad I did it this time.'

Luke's smile widened. 'I'm very, very glad that you did it this time, too.'

The party kicked up a notch as night fell and the music started.

The DJ, who was on a stage in the dining room that had been emptied of most of its tables, had clearly tried to find every great dance tune in existence and it was Georgia who was first onto the dance floor, dragging Kate along with her. It took very little time for the area to become crowded and now it was dance partners who were being exchanged instead of conversation. Kate found herself being twirled by people who spoke in languages she couldn't even identify but it didn't matter in the least because the language of dance was universal.

Eventually, she had to take a break and joined the queue at the busy bar to get a glass of water. Then she stood and watched the dancers for a while, trying to see where Georgia was. If she could spot her friend, she was going to tell her that she'd had enough. Fatigue was catching up with her and they had a very long drive to get started on in the morning.

But Georgia was nowhere to be seen on the dance floor. Or at any of the tables in here where people had gathered to listen to the music and watch the more energetic partygoers. She went outside and wandered around for a while where small groups or couples were sitting, deep in conversation near an outside bar and off to one side where a brazier was providing both warmth and an invitation to linger.

Back inside, her gaze raked the dance floor again but she couldn't see anyone she recognised, apart from Luke, who was dancing in the middle of a circle of young women. Then she saw Matteo coming towards her through a door that led to the bathrooms and exit.

'You don't know where Georgie is, do you?'

'No. I have no idea. Do you want a drink? I'm going to have one.'

'No, thanks. I've had enough. If you see her, can you tell her I've gone to bed?'

'Sure.' But Matteo was already moving towards the bar. 'See you tomorrow, Kate. Sleep well.'

'I will. You too.'

Kate stared after Matteo. Oddly, it felt like she'd said something to offend him but she didn't have time to try and figure it out. Luke came up behind her.

'Help,' he said. 'Get me away from here before I fall over. I need a rest.'

'You're not the only one. I'm heading off.'

'Oh?' Luke sounded disappointed.

'It's been amazing but if I stay any longer it won't be fun any more. I don't think I've ever been this tired in my life.'

'I'll walk you home.'

'You don't need to do that.'

'I want to.'

It was only when they got far enough away from the party that Kate realised how noisy it had been in there. There was still the background thump of the music and an occasional shout and peals of laughter but she could feel the increasing quietness and space, which made her more and more aware of the man walking beside her.

Outside the building that housed their apartments, they both stopped for a moment, caught by the view towards the mountains where a full moon was rising above the jagged peaks.

With a sigh of pleasure, Kate finally turned away.

'See you tomorrow, Luke. Or, if we miss you, I'll see you back in Scotland.'

'I'll look forward to that.' Luke was smiling. 'Goodnight, Katy.'

It was only natural to hug such a good friend to say goodnight. But maybe it wasn't so natural for the hug to go on for quite so long. Or for Kate to be feeling an odd stirring of sensation deep in her belly that was something quite a lot more than merely friendship should be sparking.

Startled, she pulled back but Luke's arms didn't loosen their hold and so she found herself looking up at his face that was so close she could feel his breath on her skin.

Stopping any further effort to pull away might have been a mistake. Catching his gaze definitely was because she'd never seen Luke looking at her like that. As if he wanted nothing more than to *kiss* her?

Astonishment made her lips drift apart. It occurred to her in that heartbeat of time that that might be interpreted as an invitation but, just as instantly, she didn't care. She'd already thrown her normal caution to the wind and broken a rule or two today so why stop now, when exhaustion and possibly a little more champagne than had been wise was a perfectly good excuse?

She couldn't have said who actually initiated that kiss but she didn't care about that either. And it wasn't a passionate kiss. Just a gentle, if lingering, touch of their lips that had notes of both pleasure and total surprise.

Kate was still grappling with how surprising it had been when she finally crawled into her bed, with thoughts that were not coherent enough to be put into words rather than feelings.

The gentleness of the touch that made her remember how she'd felt when she'd seen him with that child in his arms. The background memories of a friendship she'd treasured. The resurfacing memories of how she'd felt whenever she'd been close to him in the early days of that friendship.

That flicker of attraction that had been so hard to douse.

And—so surprising that it was more than a little disturbing—the idea of having sex with Luke was no longer embarrassing at all.

The only thing that felt weird about it was that it hadn't happened a very long time ago.

It wasn't that she was about to have a teenage-style crush on him again. This felt far more real. As if it would be quite possible to actually fall in love with her old friend, she decided, as sleep finally crept up to claim her.

Maybe she was more than halfway there already...

CHAPTER FOUR

'I CAN'T BELIEVE we've been home for nearly a month.'

'I know…' Kate took the pan Georgia had finished washing and began to dry it. 'Time flies, doesn't it? And it was a bit of a struggle to get back into routine. It was almost like jet lag, the aftermath of that epic road trip.'

It shouldn't have been that hard to embrace her normal routine, however. Kate loved routine. Had the struggle been caused by an element of distraction? Because she had found her thoughts occupied by Luke so often? It had only taken a few days for the weariness of the long journeys and intense competition to wear off but even then, it was more than post-excitement fallout that had made Kate feel a little flat. She was too aware of what was missing from her life. She loved her job and she had great friends but there was a hole she'd been stepping around for years now.

And, more and more as the days went past, that hole was taking on a shape that looked as if it was custom made for Luke Anderson.

'I'm still tired,' Georgia groaned, scrubbing at the handful of cutlery she held. 'Or maybe I'm bored.' Her smile was mischievous. 'If I get a callout that isn't a challenge, I want to swap it for a new scenario. Like a bus crash or a shooting incident…'

'Don't say that. What if you're tempting fate? How bad would you feel if it happened tomorrow?'

'True. Guess I'd better be grateful for all the routine chest pains and stomach aches and overdoses.' With a sigh, she dumped the cutlery onto the draining tray. 'There you go. All done. Thanks for dinner, by the way. It was great.'

'My pleasure. Your turn tomorrow. Oh, no… you're on night shift, aren't you?'

'Yep.' Georgia dried her hands on the corner of

the tea towel Kate was using. 'Hey, maybe you should go out for dinner. It's high time you and Luke got together.'

It was Kate's turn to sigh. 'We keep trying but it never works out that we've got the same time off. I can guarantee if I text him and suggest it, he'll be on call or something. We haven't been able to manage a coffee since we've been back, let alone a whole day's sightseeing.'

'Make it happen,' Georgia said. 'You never know—it could change your life.'

'You want to know something?'

'What?'

Kate felt her lips curl into a smile that felt hopeful. 'I think you might be right.'

'*Aha...* I knew it...' Georgia grinned back at her. 'You've been so quiet lately. You're really keen on him, aren't you?'

'We were such good friends, way back. I... I might have even had a bit of a crush on him.'

'No way...really?'

'It was short-lived. I got over it as soon as I realised he wasn't interested in me like that.' Kate bit her lip. Yes, she'd got over it fast enough but there had always been that remnant. That knowledge that this friendship had an element that made it unique. She let her breath out in a small sigh. 'I don't know if it could be anything more than what it always was but...'

'But you'd like it to be.'

It was a statement rather than a question and Kate found herself nodding slowly in agreement.

'So text him. Do it now.' Georgia followed Kate from the kitchen into the small sitting room of their house and watched as Kate pulled her phone from her bag.

'Oh... I've got a text.'

'From Luke?'

'Yes...' Kate could feel butterflies in her stomach as she opened the message. Good grief, she felt like a teenager who'd been waiting for *that* boy to call.

'What does it say?'

'That he's having a crazy week but has a day off on Saturday and maybe I'd like to go and find a ruined castle or look for the Loch Ness monster or something.'

Georgia laughed. 'Sounds like a perfect date.'

Kate made a face. 'Except I'm working on Saturday.' She shook her head. 'This is getting silly. Maybe it's not meant to happen.'

'Don't be ridiculous. What were the odds of you two meeting up again on a mountaintop in the Czech Republic? It was totally meant to happen.'

Kate had to smile. 'It was certainly unexpected.'

Maybe she should really make an effort this time. She could ask to swap her Saturday shift with one of her colleagues. More than one of them owed her the favour, in fact.

Her smile was getting wider. 'And it was you who had the mad idea of hooking up with someone while we were there. It was the last thing I was planning on doing.'

There was something about the way Georgia shrugged and turned away that raised Kate's suspicions. Her smile faded.

'I'm not the only one who's been a bit quiet since we got back. What aren't you talking about?'

'Nothing.'

Kate stared at her friend's back. 'You never did tell me where you disappeared to for so long during that party.'

The silence suddenly seemed charged.

'Oh, my God,' Kate breathed. 'You *did* hook up with somebody. And you never told me?'

'Wasn't much to tell.' Georgia's voice sounded tight. 'I'd rather forget about it.'

But Kate couldn't let it go like that. 'It can't have been Matteo,' she said, 'because I saw him and asked if he knew where you were and he said he had no idea.'

Georgia's expression suggested that Kate might have just beamed in from another planet. 'Why would it have been Matteo?'

'Oh, I don't know…' Kate's tone was teasing. 'Because he was gorgeous, maybe? Or because you two seemed to be getting on incredibly well?'

Georgia shrugged again. 'I guess some people

aren't okay with casual sex. I don't think I am any more either. It wasn't my best idea, was it?' She reached for the television remote. 'Let's see if there's something worth watching, shall we?'

Clearly, it was time to change the subject but Kate was frowning. It wasn't like Georgia to keep things bottled up so the experience must have been more disturbing than she was letting on. She sat down on the couch beside Georgia and gave her a quick hug.

'It's in the past now,' she said. 'And yeah…it wasn't your best idea but you'll know not to do it again. Are you okay? Really?'

Georgia nodded, hugging her back. 'I'm fine. *Really.*'

One of their favourite dramas was on but Kate couldn't get involved with the new plot twists. She was still worried about her friend. Worried about herself, too, if she was honest. She was one of the people who weren't okay with the idea of casual sex herself. Not that it would be for her if she and Luke got together but, from his point of view, it would never be anything more than a friendship with benefits.

Was she setting herself up to be in a far worse position than Georgia had been left with after her ill-advised one-off encounter? Maybe calling in a favour to get the day off on Saturday wasn't such a good idea. Given this new spin, perhaps she needed some more time to think things through. Or to let her hormones settle down or something.

She still had her phone in her hand. She hit 'reply'.

Sorry, Luke. Working on Saturday. Let's try again next week.

Luke Anderson loved his job with a passion but there were occasional moments when he knew he desperately needed more in his life.

Like right now. Here he was, on a lovely Saturday afternoon, when he could have been anywhere—doing any*thing*—that had nothing to do with the surgical management of injured children. But here he was, in his office near the paediatric intensive care unit, in Edinburgh's Royal Children's Hospital.

It was Kate's fault.

She hadn't suggested trying to swap her weekend shift with someone. She hadn't even offered a definite time that they could try again. 'Next week' felt vague enough to be a brush-off, albeit polite.

Perhaps she wasn't as keen to see him again as he was to see her?

After travelling back to Italy with Matteo and having a few days' holiday in Milan he had been later getting back to work than Kate but he'd made his first attempt to catch up three weeks ago now and it *still* hadn't happened.

With a sigh, Luke turned back to his computer screen. He had decided to prepare a case history to offer at the weekly lunch meeting next Friday, where interesting cases were presented for analysis and discussion. The little girl he'd operated on for a ruptured diaphragm and spleen was a good example of how dangerous a lap belt could be in even a relatively minor car accident and what early signs and symptoms were important to take notice of.

He'd only just set up his first slide to introduce the case when his office door burst open.

'Oh…you *are* here.' The anxious expression on the face of one of the senior nurses from PICU was morphing into relief. 'Someone said you might be.'

'What is it, Elise?'

'There's an incoming emergency. ETA about ten minutes. Eighteen-month-old boy who was climbing a table and it flipped over onto him.'

Luke's brain engaged instantly. Where had the edge of what was probably a heavy piece of furniture landed? Did the toddler have abdominal injuries or was it his chest, neck or head that had been affected?

'How much information do we have so far?'

'The mother heard the crash. He was unconscious and having a seizure when the ambulance arrived.'

Elise was already leading Luke rapidly along

the corridor towards the lifts. There was no question for either of them that he would take charge of this case, even if he wasn't officially on duty.

She pushed the button to summon the lift. 'He got to Glasgow's Eastern Infirmary thirty minutes later with a GCS of five and was intubated.'

The thought that the Eastern Infirmary was where Kate worked was only a flash of distraction. The low GCS score indicated a level of consciousness that suggested a severe injury.

'Investigations?'

'There were no obvious external injuries but they noted a mild upper body cyanosis and an ultrasound revealed a pericardial effusion.'

So it was a chest injury and there was fluid—probably blood—collecting around the child's heart. It was obvious that emergency surgery could well be needed.

The lift doors closed in front of them.

'Have we got a theatre available?'

'Yes. That was organised as soon as we got the call about the transfer. Apparently there wasn't anybody available in Glasgow for emergency chest surgery and we were going to page Colin but somebody said they'd seen you here earlier so I checked your office first.' Elise smiled up at Luke. 'If it was my kid, *I'd* want you to be looking after him.'

The compliment regarding his abilities as a paediatric trauma surgeon had a bitter-sweet edge for Luke as he recalled the moment of doubt he'd experienced only minutes ago. He put everything into his work and continued to strive towards being even better at his job—but was it at the expense of so many other things that life could offer?

The doors opened on the ground floor and they both headed past a busy reception and waiting area, through the emergency department and out through the automatic doors that led to the ambulance bay.

Only a minute later, they could hear the siren of an approaching ambulance and then it came into view. The siren was switched off but the beacons were still flashing as it stopped and then swiftly reversed towards the edge of the loading bay.

Luke could feel his adrenaline levels kick up several notches and he felt like he was the front line again—the way he had been, working with Matteo at the paramedic competition. Waiting right behind that impression was a reminder of Kate but it was easy to ignore. There was a potentially critically injured child inside this ambulance and it was real this time. If it was a blunt force injury to the little boy's heart, it would be a miracle if he was still alive but, if he was, then Luke was going to do everything in his power to save him.

The cabin of the ambulance was crowded. Luke could see the tiny child, wearing only a nappy, lying deathly still on the stretcher, surrounded by equipment like the portable ventilator, a cardiac monitor and a tangle of IV lines. A paramedic was removing oxygen tubing from the main supply to attach it to a portable cylinder. A distraught-looking woman who had to be the child's mother was holding her head in her hands and a woman dressed in scrubs had a stethoscope against the toddler's bare chest. She had her hair scraped back into a ponytail. Blonde hair.

Some tiny part of Luke's brain registered that this hair was the exact shade of Kate's hair and then the doctor straightened and turned, hooking the stethoscope back around her neck.

Of course the hair was the same shade as Kate's. It *was* Kate's.

The distraction was only the timespan of one heartbeat but Luke could feel it throughout his entire body.

Kate was here.

And it felt astonishingly *good…*

'We've got a systolic blood pressure of eighty.' The flash in Kate's eyes suggested that she was just as pleased to see Luke but she wasn't about to waste any time on personal greetings. 'He's in a sinus tachycardia of one hundred and eighty and the upper torso cyanosis is increasing.'

The ambulance crew wasn't wasting any time either. The crew member who had been driving had stepped through into the cabin and unhooked the stretcher restraints. Luke had to step to one side as they rolled the stretcher out, the wheels folding down and locking automatically as it emerged from the ambulance. He was intensely focussed now. This child was still alive...

'We're clear to bypass Emergency,' he told the crew. 'And an elevator's being held. We're heading straight for Theatre.'

The child's mother stumbled as she stepped down from the back of the ambulance in the wake of the stretcher and Luke caught her shoulder to steady her.

'Oh, my God...' she whispered, as she looked up to catch his gaze. *'Theatre?'*

'I'm Luke Anderson,' he told her. 'I'm a trauma surgeon here at the Royal and I specialise in chest injuries like this.'

They were moving now—straight through the emergency department towards the doors at the other end that led to the bank of elevators. Staff were moving obstacles like trolleys and wandering patients from their path.

'He's not going to die, is he?' the mother sobbed.

'This is all my fault… I should have been watching him more carefully…'

Kate turned her head, IV tubing in her hands as she protected a line. 'Jacob's in the best place he can be, Jennie. And with the best surgeon.'

The stretcher rattled as it went over the metal rim of the elevator and there was a moment's pause as the team manoeuvred everything to make room for people.

'Can I come with him?' Jennie begged.

'Of course you can.' Elise had been trailing the team but she stepped up now and put her hand on Jennie's arm. 'There's a place that you can wait and someone will be with you all the time. Come with me… We'll take the next lift. My name's Elise and I'm a nurse in the intensive care unit that Jacob will be going to after his surgery.'

Luke and Kate squeezed in alongside the stretcher. They were both trying to get as much information as possible by scanning readouts on the monitors and by what they could assess visually.

Luke caught Kate's glance and he could feel

his mouth tighten into grim agreement. It might be just the strong lighting in this small space but they were both thinking that the bluish tinge to Jacob's skin looked worse. The ability of his heart to function was deteriorating rapidly.

The doors opened and it was another straight line, through two sets of double doors to the suite of operating theatres. A theatre team was waiting beside an empty bed covered with a white sheet. The transfer of the tiny child was swift and smooth and the ambulance crew gathered their equipment on top of the stretcher, preparing to leave.

Luke caught Kate's glance again as the bed was rolled towards the induction room where the anaesthetist was waiting. 'Are you going to stay?'

'Can I? You don't mind if I observe?'

'You're more than welcome. Someone will find you some gear. Or there's an observation deck if you want a better view from the close-up camera. I need to go and scrub in.' But Luke paused for a brief moment as he turned away. He didn't actually smile, but he could feel the corners of his mouth soften. 'It's good to see you, Katy.'

Maybe the view wasn't as good standing at the head of the operating table, out of the way of the surgical team, but Kate was happy. She wanted to be as close as possible to this small patient whose outcome she was already so invested in. And it meant she was also as close as possible to Luke.

She watched as he entered the theatre, gloved hands crossed in front of his body to prevent any accidental touch of something not sterile, a nurse still tying the strings of his gown behind him. With a hat covering his hair, a mask over his nose and face and protective eyewear on, it could have been any surgeon coming in but Kate's body told her exactly who it was.

The tingle of anticipation—or maybe it was more like attraction—was powerful enough to actually distract Kate from everything else going on around her. It felt like an electrical current touching every cell in her body and it was emanating from a knot of sensation deep in her belly.

Yep. That was attraction. She recognised the point of origin all too well. But had she ever felt it quite this fiercely?

For a nanosecond, Kate actually thought the alarm she could hear was something internal but, in the same instant, she tapped into the acceleration of tension around her.

'He's in VF.'

The nurse painting Jacob's chest with disinfectant stopped swabbing and her forceps froze in mid-air. Kate held her breath. Ventricular fibrillation meant that the small heart had given up trying to pump blood—probably because of the pressure of the fluid trapped around it. And, if that was the case, simply delivering an external shock would not be enough to keep this little boy alive.

It seemed like time had stopped and frozen this tableau but that impression lasted for only the time it took for Kate's heart to skip a beat. And then she watched as Luke took complete control of everything with a calm confidence that took her breath away all over again.

'Scalpel, please,' he requested. 'And some blunt forceps. I'll need the saw in a second, too.'

Stepping closer to the table, he made a swift incision down the centre of their tiny patient's chest. Within a couple of minutes, the heart was visible. Using forceps, he lifted the tissue surrounding the heart in an enclosed bag and then made another incision.

'Suction, please...'

Luke was scooping clots of blood from around the small heart as his assistant angled the suction tubing.

'I can see where it's coming from,' Luke said a minute later. 'We've got a right atrial rupture here. Clamp, thanks...'

The bleeding from the heart was controlled within seconds but the heart was still not functioning.

Luke's hands were continuing to move with smooth confidence. Kate was biting her bottom lip so hard it was painful, as she watched him take hold of that tiny heart in his hand and start squeezing it with rapid compressions.

'Charge the internal defibrillators,' he ordered. 'But this may be enough...' He eased his hand out of the chest and Kate felt herself leaning forward, trying to see what the heart was doing. Was it still quivering ineffectively? Had it stopped completely? Or...?

The beep from the machine right beside her was a very different sound from the previous alarm. A single beep and then another one after a gap. And then the beeps got faster. Steadier...

'We're back in sinus rhythm,' Luke said. 'Thanks, team. Let's get this damage repaired, shall we? Suture, thanks...'

Over an hour later, Kate was still watching Luke—this time in the PICU. Jacob had been transferred there for the intensive care he was going to need for some time and Luke was using transoesophageal echocardiography to examine Jacob's heart.

'I'm happy.' His words were directed at Jennie, who was sitting on the edge of her chair, one hand holding that of her son. Jacob's father was by her side now, too, and he was holding Jennie's other hand. 'There's no sign of any residual injuries and his heart is working perfectly.'

He removed the tubing that contained the transducer at its tip from Jacob's throat and then he stripped off his gloves.

'We'll keep Jacob in here for a day or two to keep a close eye on things but then we'll wake him up and move him to the cardiac ward.'

'Is he…will he…?' Jacob's father had to stop and clear his throat and then he couldn't continue.

'I'm happy,' Luke said again, and this time he was smiling. 'I think he's going to be running around again in no time—probably giving you all the normal worry that toddlers can create—but he's come through this crisis with flying colours.'

Jacob's parents were both smiling and crying at the same time and Kate felt the prickle of her own tears.

From the moment this child had arrived in her emergency department—hours ago now—she had had very little hope of an outcome as good as this.

And it was thanks to Luke. The parents didn't need to know how close to a very different ending they had been up there in Theatre but Kate knew.

So did Luke.

His gaze met hers as Jacob's parents embraced each other.

He looked exhausted, which was hardly surprising. Kate felt like she'd just run a marathon herself and she'd only been watching, for heaven's sake.

At least he would get a break now. Jacob was under the care of an expert team who would only call Luke in if he was really needed and, the way things were looking at the moment, that was very unlikely.

They left the PICU together and walked in silence towards the elevator. Luke pushed the button and then tilted his head, one eyebrow raised as he caught Kate's glance.

'So this is what it takes to see you again? Full-on emergent cardiac surgery? Don't you think that's a bit high maintenance of you?'

Kate grinned. 'I have to say it was a very impressive performance but, no…it wasn't something I want to repeat in a hurry.'

'At least it broke the barrier.'

'Barrier?'

Luke waited for Kate to step into the lift ahead of him. 'I was beginning to think that you didn't really want to see me again.'

'Oh…' Kate could feel a flush of warmth in her cheeks, along with the flash of guilt that she had pretty much brushed Luke off in her last text. And then she looked up to see the way he was looking at her and the warmth suddenly went south.

There it was again.

That flash of a totally new kind of attraction.

'That's not true,' she said softly. 'I'm really happy to see you again.'

She couldn't look away. Neither, apparently, could Luke. They were locked in that eye contact until the elevator shuddered to a halt on the ground floor.

'How are you going to get home?' Luke asked as they walked through the reception area. 'Or do you need to go back to work?'

'I can go home. I was off duty a couple of hours ago. And I can call a taxi. My hospital will cover the cost because I came here as a medical escort.'

'Are you in a hurry?'

It only took a flash of that eye contact to set off that tingle again. No… Kate wasn't in any hurry to go anywhere away from Luke. Quite the opposite.

'Only I'm starving,' he continued. 'And I know a really nice Italian place not far from here, if you fancy having dinner with me.'

Saving a small life had been more than enough to make this a great day for Kate but, amazingly, it had just got a whole lot better.

Or maybe not.

'I can't go to a restaurant. I'm wearing scrubs.'

'This is a place that is a favourite with the staff.

They're used to people wearing scrubs. Did you bring a coat with you?'

'No. We left in kind of a rush.'

'You can use mine. I'll get changed so I won't need it.' His eyebrows were raised enough to make his face a picture of persuasion. 'Deal?'

Kate didn't need much persuasion. She was, in fact, grinning.

'Deal.'

CHAPTER FIVE

THE RESTAURANT COULD have been tucked away
on a back alley somewhere in Florence or Rome.

Heavy beams on the ceiling had trailing vines
coming from hanging baskets. The tables were
rustic and covered with checked red cloth. Slim
white candles had dribbled wax for a long time
judging by how encrusted the old wine bottle in
the centre of their small table was.

Kate had a glass of Prosecco in front of her but
Luke was filling his glass from a carafe of water.

'Just in case I get called back,' he said. 'Even
if I don't, I'll go and check on Jacob on my way
home.'

'He's going to be fine.' Kate smiled. 'You did
such an amazing job, Luke. He's one lucky little
boy.'

She knew that her admiration of how Luke had

handled such a critical case had to be written all over her face but she didn't care. He should be very proud of himself. *She* was proud of him.

'I only got to do what I did because you got him to the right place at the right time. If it had been anyone less competent receiving him in Emergency and not recognising what was going on, it would have been a very different story.'

Maybe it was the candlelight but Luke's gaze seemed just as admiring as Kate knew hers was. As if to remove any doubt, he lifted his glass to tap it gently against the edge of hers.

'Well done, you,' he said quietly.

'Well done, *us*,' Kate countered.

One side of Luke's mouth tilted upwards. 'We always were a great team, weren't we? Do you remember our first cardiac arrest?'

'How could I forget? Back in the days when you had to hold the paddles onto the chest to defibrillate and I was so scared my hands were shaking like I was holding a pair of castanets.'

She could smile about being a nervous medical student now but there was a far more lasting memory from that case. The way Luke had caught her frightened gaze as he'd paused his chest compressions to stand clear. That steady gaze had told her that she knew exactly what to do. That she could do this.

'How great was it when we got him back?'

'It was the best.' Kate took a long sip of her wine. 'And do you remember the kid that bit your finger?'

Luke laughed. 'I think I still have a scar.'

Kate was laughing, too. 'The look on your face! It was priceless.'

'It was a lesson I've never forgotten. I protect my fingers at all times now.'

'Didn't put you off working with kids, though.'

'Ah…but I keep them unconscious most of the time. I find it easier not to get bitten that way.'

Memories—and laughter—were easy to find as they shared an antipasti platter of calamari and olives and then deep dishes of the restaurant's signature lasagne that came with a fresh green salad and slices of crusty bread. It was only when they both sighed with pleasure over the first taste of the tiramisu they had both ordered for dessert that Kate realised something unusual.

'Do you know, this is the first time I've ever been to a restaurant when someone else has ordered exactly the same things I did.'

'That's bad, isn't it? It means you don't get the chance to taste something different.'

'No, no…it's good. I get terrible food envy.'

Luke grinned. 'You mean when you see what someone else has ordered and it suddenly looks so much better than what you chose?'

'Exactly.'

He was still smiling. 'We always did like the same things pretty much, didn't we? Same music, same movies.'

'Same friends, same careers…' Kate couldn't look away from that smile. The way his eyes crinkled at the sides. The warmth she could feel that came from knowing how intelligent this man was. How funny he could be. How caring she knew he was.

And then she remembered that kiss in the moonlight up in the mountains of the Czech Republic and the warmth twisted into something a heck of a lot more powerful.

Powerful enough to take her breath away.

Their friends had been right, all those years ago. She and Luke *were* perfect for each other. Why on earth hadn't Luke seen it before he'd met Nadia? Before it had been too late?

Luke had raised his glass again.

'To friendship,' he offered.

The toast was welcome because it gave Kate a much-needed gulp of her wine. Friendship wasn't what was making her blood sing right now. It couldn't account for the delicious knot of desire in her belly or the way her heart was being squeezed so hard it almost hurt.

This…

This was falling in love.

No. It was worse than that.

It wasn't falling. It was the moment when you hit the ground *having* fallen.

Maybe it had happened back at the competition. Or sometime over the last few weeks when she'd been thinking about Luke so often. Or maybe it had always been there and she'd just been trying to protect her heart by dismissing it as no more than a passing physical attraction. A silly crush…

Surely Luke could feel that something huge had just changed between them?

But he was busy scraping the last delicious morsels from his dessert plate. And then he glanced up and saw that Kate was watching.

'So much better than falling in love, isn't it?'

'Huh…?' For a heart-stopping moment, Kate thought he'd been reading her mind.

'Friendship.'

'Oh…' Kate blinked. She tried to smile. He hadn't noticed anything different, then.

Because he wasn't looking?

No. It was more likely because he'd never felt the same way. And never would.

'Especially this kind of friendship,' Luke continued. 'The kind that lasts for ever. It's what you'd hope you could have if you fell in love with the right person. After all the crazy stuff wears off.'

Kate swallowed hard. 'But what's wrong with the crazy stuff?'

She could feel a good dose of it herself right now, making her hyperaware of everything around her. The flicker of the candlelight, the rich smell of good food. Of how impossibly gorgeous Luke Anderson was. She couldn't take her eyes off him as he finished scraping the last of his dessert onto his spoon and lifted it to his lips. She could imagine those hands on her skin. Those lips on hers. The way he ran his tongue over his lips after the spoon had delivered its prize was the last straw. Desire was spiralling into something that felt out of control.

Feeling out of control was so alien to Kate she was sure she shouldn't be liking it at all. Not this much, anyway.

'It doesn't last.' Luke's clipped tone was like a splash of cold water. More than enough to halt that spiralling sensation. 'And you can't trust it, believe me.' His eyes narrowed. 'Are you going to eat the rest of your tiramisu?'

'Um…no.' Her appetite for the sweet treat had

somehow vanished in the last few minutes. 'I've had enough. Here…' She pushed her plate towards him and the ease with which Luke accepted the gesture underlined everything they had between them. A closeness that could be tapped back into so easily. Like family…

But he was wrong. Okay, he'd been burned but so had she in the past, albeit that she'd never gone as far as marrying someone. You couldn't give up on something like being in love. If you found the right person, this feeling could last a very long time. Maybe for ever, if you were really lucky.

Kate believed in it. She trusted it. But she couldn't tell Luke that. And she certainly couldn't tell him that it was exactly the way she was feeling. If he even got a hint of it, that easy familiarity between them would vanish. He might convince himself that even friendship couldn't be trusted either and there would never be any more times like this. She might try and text him to set something up but he would always be unavailable. Working. Or simply wary.

'So…it's the sensible thing to do, isn't it?'

'Sorry?' Had she been on another planet while Luke was polishing off her dessert and had missed something he'd said?

Luke put his spoon down.

'To marry someone that you're already great friends with.'

'Oh, no…' Kate put her hands over her eyes. 'This is about that pact again, isn't it?'

'Is it such a crazy idea?'

Kate dropped her hands, her eyes widening. *'Yes.'*

'Why?'

'You can't just marry someone because they're a *friend*…' The concept was shocking. Why would anyone give up on the idea of finding true love that swept everything else into complete shade?

But Luke seemed to be taking this idea seriously. 'Why not? Seems like a pretty good place to start, if you ask me. You always hear people say "I married my best friend".'

Kate could feel furrow lines appearing on her forehead. 'Yes, but…'

'But what?'

'But they have more than that to begin with. You've got to have more than that.'

'Such as?'

Kate could feel colour creeping into her face now. 'Um…attraction?'

Luke leaned towards her. His eyes had a mischievous glint and his mouth had a cheeky curl on one side. 'You don't think I'm attractive? Are you saying I'm ugly?'

'No…' Her cheeks were on fire now. Her body was telling her just how woefully inadequate her embarrassed response was. Weirdly, it was also increasing its response to Luke. Maybe it was that glint in his eyes. Or that smile. He was not only incredibly attractive but he would probably be *fun* in bed, too.

Oh, help…there was that out-of-control sensation again. Sucking her in and hurling her into that spiral of desire.

'And you're gorgeous,' Luke said softly. 'No red-blooded male wouldn't find you attractive.'

Kate's head was spinning now. He found her

attractive? He *wanted* her…? With a desperate effort, she tried to find a sane corner of her brain.

'It's not just about looks. There's got to be… um…chemistry.'

'Ahh…' Luke sat back in his chair, nodding slowly. 'I get it. You mean the sexual compatibility thing.'

Kate had to close her eyes for a moment so that she could concentrate on breathing. There didn't seem to be enough air in here any more. Her cheeks still felt hot. Good grief, what if someone at a nearby table was listening in to this extraordinary conversation?

Her eyes snapped open. 'Can we go now?'

'Sure.' Luke still seemed perfectly relaxed as he signalled that he was ready for the bill.

'I'll wait outside for you. I could do with a bit of fresh air.'

The air was fresher than she'd expected and Kate pulled on Luke's heavy, wool-lined anorak she had grabbed from the peg on her way out. It was far too big for her but it was warm and… she wrapped her arms around herself and let her chin sink so that her nose was buried in the lining…it smelt like Luke. All macho and masculine and…totally delicious.

She was so lost in the moment that she didn't hear Luke coming up behind her. Wasn't aware of him until she heard the low growl of his voice right beside her ear.

'I think we'd be very compatible.'

Oh… Lord… She'd always thought that women in books going weak at the knees was verging on ridiculous but it *was* actually a thing.

Instinctively, she lifted her head to turn towards that compelling growl and Luke's fingers captured her chin. In slow motion, he tilted his head and closed the gap between them. Kate knew he was going to kiss her and now her brain felt just as weak as her knees. She couldn't have stopped this happening if her life depended on it.

Because she didn't *want* to stop it happening.

That gentle kiss under the moonlight weeks ago had been laced with pleasure and surprise.

This one was a revelation.

It ignited a level of desire that she'd never

dreamed she was capable of feeling. She'd certainly never, ever felt anything like this before. But, then, she'd never fallen in love with someone that she already knew so well. Someone she had always loved as a friend…

The combination of that shared history and trust with this newly awoken—and astonishingly fierce—attraction was stunning.

It felt old and familiar as well as being totally new and unbelievably exciting. The softness and warmth of Luke's lips, the teasing touch of his tongue, the way he was holding her face as if it was made of something precious and fragile…

Her eyes remained closed as Luke finally lifted his head.

'See?' His voice sounded a little hoarse. 'That wasn't so bad, was it?'

Kate opened her eyes. She opened her mouth, too, but no words came out.

'But it *was* only a kiss,' Luke added.

Kate blinked. *Only* a kiss? That had been the most amazing kiss ever. Had anyone else in the world ever experienced a kiss quite like that?

'So…' Luke had that glint in his eyes again. 'All we need to find out is if the rest of it works.'

Kate's voice came out in a strangled sort of croak. 'The rest of it…?'

Luke wriggled his eyebrows. '*Sex*, Katy.'

How could a single word have an effect like being hit on that vulnerable point just behind your knees? It actually felt like she was stumbling even though she was standing perfectly still. Luke must have felt her lack of balance because his arm was around her now, holding her steady. He was smiling at her. Confidently—as though he'd found the perfect answer to a problem she was having.

And perhaps he had…

Kate sucked in a deep breath. 'And…um… when do you think we should investigate that?'

His smile widened. 'No time like the present. My apartment's only a couple of blocks from here.'

Kate had already discovered that going weak at the knees was a thing. Now it seemed that your eyes could grow stalks, too.

Luke's smile faded just enough to make him look, and sound, quite sincere.

'If we give ourselves too much time to think about it, we'll find all sorts of reasons why it might not be a good idea and then it'll just get harder.' He cleared his throat and a corner of his mouth quirked. 'No pun intended.'

Kate's breath came out in a huff of laughter. This was the friend she remembered. Incorrigible but, oh, so charming...

'This is a bit weird for me, too,' Luke said quietly. 'But I really think it makes sense. We're thirty-five. We both want more in our lives than just our jobs and we know we like each other, don't we?'

Kate could only nod. He made this sound so reasonable. Sensible, even. Or was desire sabotaging her brain and looking for any excuse to allow her to do what was rapidly becoming the thing she wanted more than anything else in the world?

'More than like,' Luke continued. 'I think we

really care about each other. Trust each other. You do trust me, don't you, Katy?'

Kate swallowed hard. 'Yes.'

'Then trust me on this. It'll work.'

Of course it would work. After that kiss, Kate had no doubts whatsoever that sex with Luke would be the most amazing physical experience she would probably ever have. But what about afterwards? Would *that* work?

It might…

You couldn't really just decide to never fall in love again, could you? It either happened or it didn't—it wasn't something you could control.

Was it possible that Luke was already in love with her but he didn't recognise it yet? Possible that he would get the same kind of revelation that she had had?

That would make what they were planning to do a lot more than some kind of social experiment, wouldn't it? It would make it, well… necessary…

Luke found her hand and squeezed it. Still holding it, he turned and started walking.

And, without even a beat of hesitation, Kate followed him.

CHAPTER SIX

ONE OF LUKE ANDERSON'S favourite things in life was technology—especially when it promised to help him do his job to the very best of his ability.

'It was mind-blowing, Matt. Unbelievable.'

His friend's face filled the screen of the laptop balanced against his knees as Luke lounged on his couch, a half-empty bottle of lager in one hand.

'Four-dimensional imaging? What is that?'

Matteo also had a bottle in his hand and Skype sessions like this were almost as good as the evenings they used to share in Milan. A few drinks, some good food and company that made you want to stay up half the night, talking about anything and everything.

'It's 4D magnetic resonance imaging. You can create a 3D model of, say, the heart, with data from MRI scans at different parts in the cardiac cycle. It's not just the anatomy—you can measure and visualise blood flow in individual arteries.'

'Wow. Sounds very cool.'

'More than cool. You could actually plan a surgical procedure and know how well it's going to work before you even pick up a scalpel.'

'No way…'

'It's true. I was in with our cardiology team today to get a sneak peak. You get the 3D model, plan the corrective procedure and then you can do a blood-flow simulation to see what difference it's going to make with post-operative performance. It won't be available for a while yet but, man, it'll be a game-changer when it is. Wish I could use it on a kid we're monitoring in ICU at the moment.'

'What wrong with the kid?'

'Chest injury from a car crash. We've drained a haemothorax and are managing the lung contusion but I'm starting to suspect that there could be some damage to the aorta.'

It had been Kate's idea, when he'd discussed

his niggling concerns about the child's condition over their dinner earlier this evening.

'We've done a CT and transoesophageal echo but I'm thinking we'll run an arch aortogram tomorrow.'

'You mean today.'

'Yeah…' Luke's gaze flicked to the bottom of his screen. 'It *is* getting late. Sorry, mate. I've been talking shop for far too long. What's happening in your life?'

Matteo shrugged. 'Nothing exciting. Same old.'

'How did the date work out last week. With… um…what was her name again? That nurse?'

'Marcella. It was okay. I think she only wanted my body.'

Luke laughed. 'Lucky you.'

Matteo raised his bottle towards the camera in a toast. 'What about you? Still seeing Kate?'

'Yeah. She went home just before I called you, in fact.'

His sheets would still have the scent of her and, in a short amount of time, he would be able to slide between them and revel in the memory of their time together. The incredible smoothness of Kate's skin. The warmth of her mouth. The taste of her—which was like nothing he'd ever tasted before. So delicious. So addictive. As for the way she responded to even the merest touch of his hands or his tongue. Well…he had no words to try and describe how that made him feel but it was the best feeling ever. As if *he* was the best lover ever…

Matteo shook his head. 'No wonder you're grinning like…what is it? A cheesed-off cat?'

'Cheshire cat. And I'm not.'

'It's getting serious, man. You're spending all your free time with her. And there I was thinking you were never even going to get round to seeing her again after you got home.'

'Fate threw us together.' Luke tried to wipe a new grin off his face, but failed.

He could understand Matteo's bewilderment when it wasn't that long ago that he'd been sharing the view that it wasn't going to happen. Why had they both made it so difficult to connect? All it had needed was a bit of effort on both sides to find time to text or talk on the phone, juggling rosters to make their days off coincide and taking any opportunity to snatch an evening to share a meal—and a few hours in bed…

'So what new adventures have you been on? Another ghost tour in those creepy, underground vaults?'

'No. One was enough.'

'Bike riding?'

'No.' But hiring bicycles to explore the network of disused railway lines running past canals and through forests and tunnels was an experience worth repeating. 'We did go to a bar last week that has a ceilidh every Friday night. That was fun.'

'A kay-what?'

'It's a Scottish thing. Dancing, with someone calling out the instructions. Very social.'

'Did Georgia go too? And her boyfriend? Are you double dating?'

'No.' Matteo's tone had been casual. Too casual? Was he fishing to try and find out whether Georgia was, in fact, single? 'I haven't seen Georgia since Kate and I have been together. We meet somewhere. Or Kate comes to my place.'

'Why don't you go to hers?'

'I don't know.' Luke frowned. 'I guess because she hasn't suggested it yet.'

'Maybe Georgia disapproves.'

'Why would she do that?'

'Dunno.' Matteo was shrugging again. 'She's got some funny ideas, that one.'

'I thought you liked her.' Luke was still frowning. He had the feeling that his friend was holding back about something and that wasn't like him. And it didn't sound at all as if his friend was interested in whether Kate's flatmate was single. Quite the opposite.

'I thought I did, too. Shows how wrong you can be about some people, I guess. Hey, man. I'd better go. Early shift tomorrow.'

'No worries. Let's do it again next week.'

Matteo's easy grin also dispelled the notion that he was holding back. 'We might be doing it for real before long. Don't forget you can't get married unless I'm your best man.'

Luke was still shaking his head as he ended the call. Shutting the laptop, he lay back to rest his head on the arm of the couch.

A wedding wasn't on the cards. Sure, the 'pact' that he had resurrected was that he and Kate would marry each other if they were both still single at thirty-five but it didn't conjure up any images of a *wedding*. It was more like a general term to signify a committed relationship—the kind that you could build a future on that would be strong enough to raise a family in.

The last few weeks had been all about testing the friendship between them, hadn't it? To see if there was enough of a connection to build that future on.

Would a piece of paper make any difference to that?

No.

And he was confident that Kate would feel the same way.

Except…she was a bit of a stickler for rules, wasn't she? Maybe she would want a committed relationship legitimised by something recognisable.

Okay. Why not? A quick trip to a registry office would be doable. As long as it didn't involve any of the hoopla that went with the usual celebration of true love and happy-ever-afters.

What really mattered were the things that would last the distance. A connection that was strong enough to provide a relationship glue that would hold people together through thick and thin. And it was becoming steadily clearer that he and Kate had an endless supply of that kind of glue.

Had he really suggested to Kate that sex would only 'work'?

Man… Talk about the understatement of the century…

If Luke had had any idea of what it could be like, there was no way in the world that they would have remained simply friends back in med school.

Why on earth had he ever bought into the myth that you needed to fall in love with the person who was your perfect partner for life? That, somehow, that would make the sex better than ever?

This was the answer.

To take an established friendship to the next level. To be with someone you really liked, that you didn't have to treat like a piece of precious china that might break if you did something wrong. Someone you could be completely honest with, who knew you well enough to overlook any small wrongdoings and make them something to laugh about and learn from.

This wasn't a friendship with benefits.

This was…well…this was nothing short of perfect as far as Luke was concerned. And, best of all, Kate seemed to feel the same way. Maybe she hadn't invited him into her home yet but she'd been putting as much effort as he was into finding so much time to be together.

Matteo had called them 'adventures' and it was true that they'd been finding some very cool things to do on their days off. Like the ghost tour and the bike ride and the folk dancing. And what about that evening of pure luxury with the reclining sofas and full table service for a movie at the Dominion Theatre? That had been his idea of heaven after a full-on day.

Other couples had been holding hands or snuggling on the sofas but he and Kate didn't need that kind of mushy, romantic stuff. They were best mates when they were out and passionate lovers when they shared a bed. The absolute best of both worlds.

The ping of an incoming text message made him reach for his phone. Had Matteo thought of something else to say? He was the only person who would text him this late at night. Even Kate kept their increasingly frequent communication to more civilised hours.

But maybe that was changing because this message was from her.

Thanks for dinner. Reckon it's about time you found out how bad my cooking is. G's on night shift Wednesday if you're free.

Had Kate been waiting until Georgia was absent before inviting him to her home? The unexpected twinge of anxiety was Matt's fault. Maybe her best friend *did* disapprove and could end up talking Kate out of making a commitment to a relationship that was based on something as unromantic as a pact.

Or…maybe Kate wanted the place to themselves so that dinner could naturally morph into the kind of sexual playground that was Luke's absolutely favourite place to be these days.

Yep…that was far more likely to be the reason, given how enthusiastic Kate was to play. Tilting the bottle to finish the last swallow of lager, Luke closed his eyes in a blissful moment.

It really didn't get any better than this.

'Whoa…wasn't expecting that.'

The spell of the lingering kiss was broken at the sound of Georgia's voice but, for a heartbeat, Kate's gaze was still locked with Luke's as they drew apart.

'Want me to go out and come in again?'

A huff of laughter from Luke tickled Kate's face.

'No. We're good. I'm just leaving.' Was it her imagination or was he having difficulty dragging his gaze away from hers? 'Sorry, Georgie. I thought I'd be gone before you got back from night shift.'

'No late jobs for a change and the traffic was light.' Georgia dropped her backpack on the floor beside the kitchen door. 'You are allowed to stay here, you know, Luke.' She grinned at him. 'I've known about you and Kate for weeks so it's not exactly a secret that you're sleeping together.'

Luke was grinning back at her. 'We're just good friends.'

Georgia laughed. 'Yeah, yeah…'

Kate was trying to smile. Trying to buy into this light-hearted dismissal that anything significant had been outed but it was difficult.

Almost…heartbreaking?

How ridiculous was that? She'd just had the perfect night, in a perfect setting. A cute little cottage to themselves, a candlelit dinner for two and her own bed to share with her lover.

And that, right there, was where the problem was, wasn't it?

Luke wasn't her *lover*. He was her friend that she just happened to be having sex with. Astonishingly wonderful, passionate, even tender sex and Luke might love her in the way that you loved your best friend but to be a lover, you had to be *in love*.

Luke was gone, with a friendly wave and a promise to text Kate later in the day.

'Any tea in that pot?'

'No. The coffee's hot, though.'

Georgia shook her head, sinking onto one of the two chairs beside the tiny table tucked into the corner of the kitchen.

'I'm desperate to sleep. Coffee would keep me awake.'

'Really? You've always said it never made any difference after a night shift.'

Georgia yawned. 'Maybe I'm getting old. Or going off coffee or something.' She pulled the band off her ponytail and fluffed her hair with her fingers. 'I can make the tea. You must need to get to work, too.'

'No, I've got a later start. Long day.' Kate was filling the kettle at the kitchen sink but she was staring out of the window. Watching Luke's car as he got to the end of the driveway and turned onto the road.

Was he still thinking about her? About how perfect the night had been? Or was his mind firmly on the day ahead, perhaps going over the complex surgery he could be doing within the next hour or two on that child with a potentially damaged aorta?

The water flowing onto her hand over the top of the kettle made her realise how long she had been distracted.

'Oops…' She tipped half the contents of the kettle out.

'Not like you to be away with the fairies.' Georgia's eyebrows were raised. 'Short of sleep, huh?'

Kate shrugged. 'Maybe…'

'Ooh…do tell. I've almost forgotten what good sex is like.'

Kate was silent. She lit the gas under the kettle and then opened the cupboard to find the teabags and mugs.

'It *was* good, wasn't it? That was some kiss I interrupted...'

'Yeah...' With a sigh, Kate turned and leaned against the bench as she waited for the kettle to boil. 'It was...amazing. He's amazing. I'm...' It was disturbing how intense her voice sounded. The way it broke before trailing into silence.

Georgia's jaw dropped. 'Oh, my God... You're totally in love with him, aren't you?'

Kate closed her eyes. Her voice was no more than a whisper. 'Yeah...'

'Does Luke know? Did he say it back? Is *that* what that steamy kiss was about? Oh, help... I really did interrupt something...'

Kate shook her head. 'No. And no and no.' She opened her eyes to find her friend staring at her.

'That's a lot of "noes".'

Kate busied herself making the tea. 'I can't tell him.'

'Why not?'

'Because I'd lose him and…and I don't want to lose him.'

Georgia was frowning now. 'That doesn't make sense. From what I saw, he's totally into you.'

'As a friend.'

'Yeah…right…' The tone of disbelief echoed Georgia's reaction to Luke's claim that he and Kate were 'just good friends'. 'Who are you trying to kid?'

Kate put the mugs of tea on the table and sat down. 'There's something I've never told you. You know that Luke and I were friends back in med school?'

'Of course. He was your best friend until he got married and his wife couldn't cope with him having a girl buddy.' Georgia grinned. 'Maybe she wasn't wrong to think you might be a threat.'

'There was no attraction back then. Not on his side, anyway. And not on mine after I got over that initial crush. The idea of it would have been shocking. Like… I don't know…incest, almost. He was like my brother.'

'So when did that change so dramatically?'

'At the rally. The night of the party. He…he kissed me.'

'And now he's spending every spare minute he's got with you and giving you the best sex ever and, I have to say, he looks pretty happy about it.'

Kate nodded. 'He is. Because, as far as he's concerned, we're just friends. Because the "L" word is not an issue. For him… We made a pact, Georgie. After graduation, when we'd had too much champagne. We agreed that if neither of us was married by the time we were thirty-five—if neither of us had found "the one" we'd marry each other.'

'No way… Are you trying to tell me you're engaged?'

The headshake was emphatic. 'We haven't actually talked about that again. I tried to tell him that being good friends wasn't enough. That there had to be a different kind of connection. I was talking about being in love but he took it as meaning a sexual connection and suggested that we gave it a try and…um…' Kate bit her lip. 'I guess we're still trying that, as far as he's concerned.'

'But surely he'd be delighted if he knew how you felt. That you would be prepared to honour the pact.'

'But that's just it. He wants to reinstate the pact because we're not in love. He thinks that's the best foundation for a successful relationship. He fell in love with Nadia, remember? The first woman he married? And that was a disaster. If he knew I was in love with him, or he felt like he might be falling in love with me, he'd run a mile. He'd know he couldn't trust it.'

'Hmm…' Georgia sipped her tea. She was silent for a long time but then her gaze met Kate's steadily. 'Maybe he's right.'

'What?'

Georgia shrugged. 'You're so sure that there are rules to follow and a proper order of doing stuff but what if something like this works better? Like an arranged marriage? He might not be *in* love with you but he cares about you, doesn't he?'

Kate nodded. 'Yes. He always has. As a friend.'

'And the sex is good, right?'

Kate could feel her cheeks warming. 'Oh… yeah… I never knew it could be this good.'

And it wasn't just the sex. Last night, for the first time, they had fallen asleep together. Or rather Luke had fallen asleep and Kate had been awake for a very long time, too aware of the solid presence of his body so close to hers that she could feel as well as hear every breath he took.

It had made her feel…safe?

Protected. It wasn't that she'd ever felt nervous about being in the house alone when Georgia was on a night shift, mind you. No, this feeling of protection was about something much bigger than that.

Protection from feeling alone, perhaps. Or from a future that was emptier than she would want?

Georgia's smile suggested that she could sense what Kate was thinking about. 'Does he want the same things as you? Like kids down the track?'

'Yes, I think so. He said he wants more to life than just his career.'

'And you share the same career. You could support each other and share the kid stuff. You know what?'

'What?'

'It sounds just about perfect to me.' Georgia yawned again. 'I need to sleep.' She got up and took her mug to the sink.

Maybe she was right, Kate thought. How many women would dream of having a gorgeous guy like Luke to care about them? To have fun with. To have mind-blowingly good sex with? To be their life partner and raise a family with? Being in love wore off, everybody knew that. Eventually, the lucky ones were left with…well, pretty much what she and Luke had now.

Georgia was still standing beside the sink. Staring into it, presumably at the dirty breakfast plates that probably had congealed egg fragments all over them.

'I'll do the dishes in a minute.'

But Georgia didn't seem to hear her. She had

her hand pressed against her mouth and when she turned away from the sink, her face was pale. Very pale.

Shocked, Kate watched her run from the room. Their small, downstairs bathroom was right beside the kitchen so it was impossible not to hear her throwing up. Especially seeing as Kate followed her. A few minutes later, she was offering a damp facecloth as Georgia finally sat back on her heels and let go of the hair she had been holding back from her face.

'I'll never eat eggs again in my life,' she groaned.

'You didn't eat any in the first place. You just looked at the plates.'

'I know…' Georgia leaned back against the wall, the facecloth pressed against her eyes.

'Are you sick? Running a temperature?' Kate reached for her friend's wrist, to check her heart rate.

'I don't think so.'

'Did you eat something dodgy on night shift? Like a kebab?'

'No.'

Something was nagging at the back of Kate's brain as it collected all available information. Georgia had looked tired but not unwell when she'd arrived home. She hadn't wanted coffee because she said it might keep her awake. Or that she'd 'gone off it'. The nausea had been triggered by the sight of egg yolk.

'Oh, my God…' Kate could feel the colour of her own face fading. 'Are you pregnant. Georgie?'

Georgia didn't respond. She seemed, in fact, to have gone very, very still.

Kate sank onto the bathroom floor and shuffled around so that she was leaning against the same wall as Georgia. It was her sigh that broke the long silence.

'When were you going to tell me?'

'When it was too late to have an argument about whether or not it was a good idea to go through with it.'

Kate's breath came out in a shocked huff. 'Did you think I'd try and persuade you to have a termination?'

Georgia lowered the facecloth. Damp curls framed hazel eyes that seemed a lot bigger than usual. 'Why not? You've never approved of my plan for single parenthood. You told me the whole idea was hare-brained.'

'That doesn't mean I wouldn't support you in whatever you chose to do.' Kate could feel tears prickling at the back of her eyes. 'I can't believe you've kept this to yourself. How pregnant *are* you?'

'About ten weeks.'

Kate's brain had no trouble doing the maths. 'So it was the person you hooked up with at the rally. Who was it?'

'It doesn't matter.'

'Of course it matters. It's your child's father. You need to know about family genetics. You'll need financial support.'

Georgia's headshake was emphatic. 'That's precisely the reason I did it this way. I don't want to know about the father's family. I don't want financial support. I don't want anyone interfering in any way. This is *my* baby. And it's going to stay that way. Don't ask again, Kate, because I'm never going to tell you. I'm never going to tell anyone, *especially* the father. And I couldn't anyway because I don't have his address. I barely remember his name. And…oh, *God*… I'm going to be sick again…'

The vomiting almost seemed an appropriate finale to the impassioned speech. It was some time after that before the atmosphere in the small house felt calmer. Georgia tried another cup of tea and a piece of dry toast and declared herself to be over the bout of morning sickness.

'I'm going to sleep like a log.'

'Are you on another night shift?'

'Yes.'

'Should you even be working at the moment? Aren't there rules about being pregnant and on the road?'

Georgia sighed. 'Yes. And I'll sort that soon but I'm not looking forward to getting stuck behind a desk on light duties. I'm fine, honestly. I'm being careful about lifting and everything. It's not as if my body's not used to this stuff. It's only dangerous if you're doing different things—like riding a horse for the first time. The women that are used to it can ride safely pretty much until they give birth.'

'But there are rules. They're there for a reason.'

Georgia rolled her eyes. 'Cut it out, Kate. I'm a big girl. I get to make my own decisions.' She stood up. 'And right now I'm deciding that it's my bedtime. Have a great day.' She grinned at Kate. 'How could you not, after having such a great night?'

Shock waves were still ebbing around Kate as she drove to work an hour or two later.

Georgia had gone ahead with her crazy scheme not to miss out on being a mother and she was choosing to do it entirely on her own.

It was still beyond anything Kate could imagine doing and she had to admire her friend's courage and determination.

And no wonder Georgia thought that her relationship with Luke offered the perfect compromise. A partnership built on friendship and equality and trust. The idea of heartbreak or 'interference' seemed a million miles away.

On paper, Kate had to agree.

It sounded just about perfect.

So why didn't it *feel* perfect?

Maybe she needed to take a leaf out of Georgia's book. Absorb a bit of that courage and determination and let go of what her friend considered her ridiculous 'rose petal and bluebirds' mentality.

And then it really hit home.

Georgia was *pregnant*. She was going to have a baby and be a mother. She was choosing to create her own family and give herself the future she wanted.

The kind of future that Kate wanted, too.

The kind that was within touching distance, even. With the added bonus of someone to share it with. Someone who would care about her and support her and…and be an amazing father.

Georgia was right.

Luke was right.

Friendship was what mattered.

And this was as perfect as it was ever likely to get.

CHAPTER SEVEN

'I CAN'T SEE any monsters.'

'Neither can I.'

'It's beautiful…' Kate snuggled closer beneath the arm around her shoulders as she stared out at the glimmering expanse of Loch Ness. 'Bit cold, though.' She glanced up at a leaden sky. 'I think it's going to rain very soon.'

Luke didn't seem to hear her warning. He was shading his eyes with his free hand despite the lack of sunshine. 'Look…did you see *that*?'

'What?'

'There… No, *there*… I saw something.'

'Something long and smooth?' Kate's lips were curving upwards. 'Bit like a giant serpent, perhaps?'

'Exactly. You saw it, too?'

'No. And neither did you.' But the glint of mischief in Luke's eyes made her smile widen. Made her feel suddenly, inexplicably, enormously happy.

'Ah, Katy…' His sigh was theatrical. 'You know me too well.'

But Luke was smiling, too, holding her gaze, and Kate could feel something in the moment change. Maybe it came through the arm still slung over her shoulders. Or maybe it was simply the way he was looking at her. Was he about to kiss her? When the touch would be about something very different from sex?

She felt her heart skip a beat. If he did kiss her right now, it would give her hope that there could be more to this than a 'friends with benefits' thing. There was certainly something much deeper than amusement in that gaze. A familiarity laced with the sheer pleasure of each other's company perhaps. A connection that felt—in that moment—unbreakable.

Had Luke, at some subconscious level, recognised the shift in Kate's attitude to their relationship? That she was on board with the resurrection of their pact? That she realised now that what

Luke could offer was actually better than the fairy-tale of being head over heels in love with someone who felt exactly the same way?

She couldn't hold the eye contact, however, in case he could see that this was a deliberate choice to hide how she really felt.

What she *really* wanted… So much that it sent a tiny shudder through her body.

'You're freezing.' Luke moved, taking Kate with him as he turned towards where they'd parked the car. 'Let's find a pub and feed you.'

The crackling fire they found to sit beside a short time later was such a change of scene that Kate found herself pausing before she dipped her spoon into her very welcome bowl of hot soup.

Here she was, warm and being cared for. Would she really rather still be standing beside a romantic, misty lake—being kissed senseless by someone who also hadn't noticed how cold it was?

She could almost feel Georgia poking her. No, of course she wouldn't. That was the stuff of idealistic, teenage girls. It wasn't real life.

'You don't feel like soup?' Luke had noticed her hesitation. 'Want to order something else?'

'No. Soup's great. I was just thinking.'

He grinned. 'Did it hurt?'

'Has anybody ever told you that sometimes you lack a certain maturity?'

His nod was solemn. 'Quite often. What were you thinking about?'

'Georgia.' The honest response slipped out.

'Oh…she was put out to find me in the house when she got home the other day, wasn't she?'

'Not at all. She's got more important things than my love-life to think about at the moment.'

'Like what?'

'She's…um…pregnant.'

'So she *does* have a boyfriend.'

'Not exactly.' Kate bit her lip. The pregnancy wasn't a secret given that everybody would know about it soon enough. But the intentional conception and the determination to keep the baby's father out of the picture was definitely a private matter and Kate would never betray her friend.

Even to someone she trusted as much as Luke. 'What makes you think that?'

'Something Matt said. I guess she might have told him that there was someone else. I also think that he might have been a bit disappointed.' Luke's glance was quizzical. 'I got the impression they quite liked each other.'

'Mmm. Me, too.' Kate was concentrating on her soup now. Had the chosen target already been identified amongst the crowd of contenders at the competition when Georgia had told Matteo that there was someone else? It was just as well she *hadn't* chosen Luke's friend as her sperm donor. Imagine how complicated that could make things?

'Is she happy about it?'

'About what?'

She got a slightly bewildered glance this time. 'About being pregnant. Being a solo parent.'

'Ah…yes, I think she is. Her biological clock starting sounding an alarm a while back.'

Luke reached for another slice of the crusty bread in the basket. 'How's your clock?'

'Ticking. No alarms bells yet.'

'But you want kids?'

Kate nodded slowly. 'Yeah… I would certainly like to think of a family in my future.'

Luke caught her gaze. 'Me, too.' He smiled at her. 'How many?'

'At least two.'

'Girls or boys?'

'One of each?'

'Perfect.' Luke was smiling again. 'When do you want to get started?'

'Um… I hadn't thought quite that far ahead.' The next few months were enough to be dealing with. How things would pan out between herself and Luke. And now, watching Georgia go through each stage of this pregnancy until she was holding her newborn baby in her arms.

Kate caught her breath. Imagine that…

'The rate of complications goes up after you hit forty,' Luke said, matter-of-factly, dipping his bread into his soup. 'So does the ease of conception.'

'True.' Kate took another spoonful of her soup,

marvelling at how they could be having a conversation like this and eating their lunch as if it
was nothing out of the ordinary.

'So you probably want to have both of these
well-planned babies before you hit the big Four-
Oh, yes?'

'I guess.'

'And nobody gets pregnant on their first attempt.'

'I think Georgia did.'

'Do you know how rare that is? Some perfectly
normal couples take a year to conceive.'

For the next few minutes they both ate in silence. Luke finished first, wiped his mouth with
his paper napkin and sat back against the stuffed
leather of the armchair.

'Right. I've done the maths.'

'Oh?'

'Two kids, with the apparently ideal gap of two
years between them and preferably born before
you hit the next decade. Allowing for a possible
year for conception that brings us to…ooh, let's
see…right about now.'

Kate's spoon settled into her almost empty bowl with a distinct clatter. She was doing her best to fully embrace the idea of committing to a long-term relationship with Luke even if he wasn't—and possibly would never be—in love with her, but this… This was a huge new step along that track.

'You want to try for a *baby*?'

'Why not?' Luke reached across the table and caught her hands. 'We've proved this can work, haven't we? We like each other—a lot. The sex is…well, it's amazing for me.'

The skin contact of his hands on hers was enough to send tingles up Kate's arms to spread throughout her entire body. The extra squeeze only accentuated them.

'For me, too,' she murmured. Hopefully no one else in this quiet country pub was near enough to be overhearing this conversation.

'Do you remember what I told you the night we made that pact?'

'I have to admit that parts of it a bit blurry. It

was a long time ago, Luke. And we'd both had a lot to drink.'

'Yeah…oddly, though, I remember a lot of it very clearly. I remember telling you that you were my best mate and I loved you to bits.' Luke's voice was also low. Intense, even. 'That doesn't seem to have changed. Right from when I saw you at the rally, it felt like things were just the way they always were between us. We both want the same things out of life. So…why *not*?'

'Um…' Oh, help. He'd said the 'L' word and, even though it had been delivered under the guise of friendship and was therefore perfectly acceptable, it was doing weird things to Kate. It was exactly what she'd dreamed of hearing but…but not like *this*…

For one horrible moment she thought she might cry.

Luke was watching her, a furrow between his brows. 'Is it because we're breaking rules, Katy? Your rules?'

Kate swallowed hard. 'We're talking about the rest of our lives, Luke. About…about a *family*…'

'Ah… I get it.' Luke nodded slowly. 'It's too much to think about having kids together if we're not married, right?' He smiled at her. 'It's okay. I know I said I'd been there and done that and I was over the whole marriage thing but I really only meant picking your partner by the crazy, totally unreliable, 'falling in love' business. I'm happy to marry you. It's just a visit to a registry office to sign some papers after all.'

Kate couldn't breathe. This had morphed into a *proposal*? One that was so far from being the romantic declaration she would have wished for herself, it triggered a sharp and totally unexpected pang in her chest. Was it actually physically possible for a little bit of your heart to break?

'You guys all done?' The cheerful voice of the waitress was a rude reminder that this wasn't the place for a conversation like this.

Except…maybe it was.

Like everything else about this relationship, it was based on common sense and openness and trust and there was nothing wrong with any of

those things. Quite the opposite. Okay…maybe
this wasn't the way that Kate had wanted it to
happen but she was going to end up with exactly
what she'd dreamed of, wasn't she? A future with
someone she loved with all her heart.

A family. Maybe a lot sooner than she had expected.

Summoning a somewhat shaky smile, she nodded at the waitress.

'Thank you. Yes, I think we're all done.'

But when the plates had been cleared away and
Kate caught Luke's gaze, ready to agree that a
registry office wedding would be fine by her, she
couldn't do it.

As friends, this idea of creating such a strong
partnership that they could raise a family together was acceptable.

But marriage? A *wedding*?

That was too bound up in her head and her
heart with the concept of celebrating love in public. Of making pledges in front of others that
were heartfelt and genuine. And…okay, maybe it
was immature. Silly, even, but the traditions were

significant, too. The white dress. The vows and the music and the party afterwards. An aisle to walk slowly down as you got closer and closer to the person who mattered more than anyone else in the world. Someone she was totally and absolutely in love with—who felt exactly the same way about *her*...

Perhaps it was a stretch to think of a 'quick visit to a registry office' as a wedding but it would be the only one she would ever have, wouldn't it? But if she was patient, maybe one day Luke might feel differently? Might see her as more than a friend or the potential mother of his children? That would be when she would want to consider a wedding—not now...

And...maybe knowing that a baby was a possibility would be a trigger for Luke to feel differently?

As he'd pointed out himself, it could take a long time to get pregnant so maybe giving up the protection they'd been using would be the first step to encourage Luke towards that change.

Her gaze slid away from his.

'We don't need a wedding, do we? Or a piece of paper to legitimise things?' Somehow, she even summoned a shrug. 'It's not as if we needed a written version of the pact to make it work.'

A quick glance showed how surprised Luke was looking. Impressed, even?

'That's true.' His smile had that cheeky edge she loved. 'Hey, if you're prepared to break the rules, count me in. But...'

'But?'

'I don't know... You might change your mind. It's a break with tradition that seems more like something I'd do than you would.'

'Maybe I'm getting older and wiser.'

'Hmm. And maybe you might change your mind. Why don't I see what's involved? How much paperwork it might take. Just in case.'

Another shrug was easy to find. 'Sure. But only if you want to. I'm not that bothered.'

'And the baby thing? You want to give that a go?'

Would it be totally irresponsible to take a risk like that? To break such big personal rules in the hope that the odds were in her favour and that it would take enough time for Luke to have some kind of epiphany when the possibility of becoming a father became increasingly real?

Kate was still riding the wave of that last shrug. 'Why not? It's not going to change anything anytime soon, is it? When—or if—it happens, I'm sure we'll be ready for it.'

'I'm late.'

'So am I. And there's no way I'm going to get these pants done up.' Georgia was struggling to get her buttonhole near the button but there was an obvious gap of a couple of inches. 'What am I going to do? I'm never late to work.'

'No. I mean I'm *late…*'

Georgia let go of her waistband, her eyes widening. 'You don't mean *late* late?'

Kate could only nod.

'How late?'

'A week.'

'That's nothing. Could be stress.'

'I'm as regular as clockwork. And it fits.'

'Fits with what?'

'When we decided not to bother with protection any more.'

Georgia's mouth was as wide as her eyes now. 'You *planned* this?'

'Not exactly. We both thought it would take ages. It never happens the first time.'

'It did with me.'

'I know.' Kate stared at Georgia's unfastened waistband. Would her belly be expanding inexorably like that in a few months' time?

With a *baby* growing inside her?

The thought was mind-blowing.

Confusing. Scary. But there were definitely tendrils of excitement trying to take hold.

'Okay.' Georgia's breath came out in a decisive huff. 'First of all, you need to find out. I've got a spare test kit or two in my room.' She grinned at Kate. 'I bought a bulk supply.'

'I could get a blood test at work.'

'Don't you want to know now?'

'I'm not sure.' Kate's gaze drifted back to Georgia's current problem. 'I reckon a safety pin would do the trick for now. Can you find a bigger pair at work?'

'Yes. But don't change the subject. Have you told Luke?'

'Not yet. I'm seeing him tonight.'

'Maybe you could do the test together?'

'Sounds like a fun evening.' Kate bit her lip.

Would Luke be as shocked as she was at the possibility of life changing so dramatically in the near future? She'd certainly know how committed he was to the idea of taking the pact to the ultimate conclusion, wouldn't she? Whether or not the test was positive, she'd see exactly how he really felt about it in a heartbeat. In the moment he raised his gaze to hers, having looked at that little window on the stick.

'But it's not a bad idea.' Kate smiled at Georgia. 'How 'bout you find the kit for me and I'll find you a safety pin?'

No way…

It couldn't be this easy, surely?

To have found the perfect partner and then to

plan on starting a family and have it happen just like that?

He was going to be a *father*?

Luke didn't need the odd prickle behind his eyes to tell him how huge this was. The emotion was so overwhelming he couldn't think of a thing to say when he raised his gaze from the stick to look at Kate.

But maybe he didn't need to say anything. Kate was looking pretty misty herself. And...vulnerable?

Had she thought he might not be happy about this? Freaked out, even?

With the stick still in his hand, he gathered her into his arms and held her tightly. Then he pressed a kiss against her hair.

'I should have known.' He smiled. 'Set you a challenge and you have to exceed all expectations, don't you? Do better than anyone else.'

'I think we did this one together.' Kate tilted her head up. 'You're really happy about this, aren't you?'

'I'm thrilled. Aren't you?'

'I'm…a bit shocked, to be honest. I thought I had months to get used to the idea. To plan what to do about taking time off work and…and where we're going to live.' She pulled back from Luke. 'Where *are* we going to live? We work in different cities. This apartment's far too small and I can't ask Georgia to move out of our house— she's the one who took the lease. And she's already planning how it's going to work after *her* baby arrives.'

'How much do you love Glasgow?'

'I love my job.'

'Me, too. But I've always loved my job—it doesn't seem to matter where.'

'You mean you might want to shift?'

'I mean anything's possible. We could go anywhere, Katy. Anywhere in the world. We're going to be parents.' Luke blew his breath out in an astonished huff. 'How amazing is that? We could choose the best place on earth to bring up a family and make it happen.'

'Is there a best place?'

'I reckon. Somewhere that has a lot of sunshine,

maybe. And beaches. Good schools and excellent hospitals. Australia?'

Kate's jaw dropped. 'You can't be serious.'

'No.' But Luke's lips were curving into a wide smile. Man, the possibilities suddenly opening up were exciting. 'I think New Zealand would be even better. I've got a friend who emigrated a few years back and he reckons it's the only place in the world he'd want to be raising his family.'

Kate shook her head. 'You're crazy.'

'*This* is crazy. But it's happening.' Luke pulled her back into his arms and spun them around with a few impromptu dance steps. 'We've chosen each other. We've chosen to start a family. Why not choose a whole new life? A new beginning for the rest of our lives?'

Excitement was morphing into an astonishing flash of happiness. This was so much better than anything he'd factored into his life plan. Because he could trust it? Kate was never going to break his heart. They had chosen to be together like sensible adults who knew that friendship was the only reliable base for a relationship. She felt exactly the same way he did about it and she was prepared to totally commit herself. The proof of that was in that little plastic stick he still had in his hand.

He let the stick drop as he brought the dance to a halt. He shifted his hands so that he was holding Kate's head between them and then he bent to kiss her. A long, slow kiss that she responded to the way she always did—as if she was melting into his arms.

He loved that. He loved it that you could be no more than the best of friends and that sex could be better than ever.

And he loved it that a whole new phase of life was taking shape around him—like ripples spreading out from a thrown pebble. He was that pebble.

No. He *and* Kate were. All these new possibilities were only there because they were together. A new home. Maybe in a new place. A real home, with a whole family of his own.

This was exactly why he'd had that epiphany that resurrecting their pact wasn't such a silly idea. When he'd realised just how much he loved kids, as he'd watched them scrambling for the sweets and gifts during that convoy at the end of the competition. After that moment he'd had with the little boy who'd been a part of that bus-crash scenario.

Everything was suddenly falling into place, far more easily than he would have believed possible.

Thanks to Kate.

He had to break the kiss. Before it spiralled into something that would make him forget anything else for quite some time.

'Thank you,' he whispered aloud.

Kate's eyes drifted open. She was blinking up at him as if it was difficult to focus.

'What for? Getting pregnant?'

Luke smiled down at her. 'For being you. For being my best friend. For not...' He wasn't sure exactly what he was trying to put into words now.

He could feel her body tensing as it came out of that melted state. Her eyes had darkened, too. They looked clear now. Piercing almost.

'For not falling in love with you?'

Luke closed his eyes, his breath coming out in a sigh of relief. 'Exactly. This isn't crazy stuff we can't trust. We both want this so we know it's going to work.'

'Mmm…' She was pulling away from him slowly. 'Well, it's in the fine print, isn't it?'

Luke frowned. There was something in her tone that he couldn't identify. Something that bothered him, even though Kate was smiling.

'The pact?' Kate stooped to pick up the pregnancy test stick that he'd dropped. 'We made it because we were friends. If that changed, it wouldn't work, would it?'

'Mmm.' Oddly, his tone was an exact echo of Kate's. A little off-key? Something was bothering her. But what?

He watched her drop the stick into the rubbish bin. 'Is it too early for me to have a craving for something, do you think?'

He couldn't see her face at the moment, but her voice sounded perfectly normal again. Light-hearted even.

'Depends what it is…' He knew what he wanted.

To kiss her again and take her into his bed. To forget about everything else for the rest of the evening.

'Nachos.' Kate turned and grinned at him. 'That Mexican restaurant round the corner has the best nachos ever.'

'Takeout or eat in?'

'Takeout,' Kate said. 'That way you'll have your laptop handy. You can show me everything I don't know about New Zealand.'

'Wow…you'd really consider that?' Every time he thought he knew this woman so well, she had another surprise in store for him.

He loved that about her, too.

'Well… So far, you've persuaded me to buy into the pact and give up on my lifelong dream of being swept off my feet by a grand passion. Now we're actually going to have a *baby*.' There was a brightness in her eyes that suggested tears might not be far away but she was still smiling. 'I'd say the chances of talking me into starting a new life on the opposite side of the world are pretty good, wouldn't you?'

Was this what was bothering Kate at some level? How much of what was changing in their lives was about persuasion and how much was what Kate was really happy to be doing?

Had she brushed off the idea of getting married because she thought that was what he'd prefer? He had dismissed marriage along with the idea of ever falling in love again when they'd first reconnected but maybe it was more important to Kate than he realised. Especially with a baby on the way. Had she been hiding how she really felt?

'You know how I downloaded those forms about registering an intention of getting married?'

Kate was putting on her coat, ready to go out and get their dinner. 'Yeah. I had no idea you couldn't just rock up to a registry office and do the deed.'

Luke picked up his own coat. 'I think we should sign them. Just in case.'

'In case of what?'

'In case we…oh, I don't know…decide that it

would be better for our kid to have married parents. Or if we decided to emigrate and suddenly find it's a whole lot easier to be legally a couple. It's not as if we have to set an actual date or anything yet. I'd leave that up to you. Whatever *you* want.'

A flash of something crossed Kate's face and Luke was certain that he was right. She had been hiding something and he was doing the right thing here, by giving her some options. Control even.

He couldn't be entirely sure but she looked a bit more relaxed.

'Okay. Thanks.' She was smiling again. '*Now* can we go and get some food?'

The lights were on in every corner of this paediatric ward of Glasgow's Eastern Infirmary, even though it was the middle of the morning.

Kate glanced through a blurred window at the heavy, grey sky.

'It's raining. Again.'

'That's Scotland for you.' Her registrar was

leading the way to the next patient on their ward round.

'How long have you been here?'

'Two years. But I've applied for a job back home and I've got my fingers crossed. They're short of paediatricians in New Zealand at the moment.'

'So I hear…' Kate smiled at the young mother sitting cross-legged on the bed with a baby on her lap. 'Hi, Janet. Oh, my goodness…you're looking happy this morning, Muriel!'

It was such a grown-up name for the three-month-old and, along with the bright red curls on her head and the cutest button nose, it made her smile every time. Especially now, when Muriel had come through a terrifying battle with pneumonia but had now been out of Intensive Care for several days.

And she was such a smiler. Kate only had to touch the tiny nose or make a surprised face and the baby's mouth curved into a grin that seemed to go from ear to ear.

'She still sounds a wee bit wheezy. I'm going

to have a good listen to her chest now. How's her feeding going?'

'She's still getting a bit tired so I have to do it little and often. I'm so happy to be breastfeeding again, though.'

'It's so much better for both of you.' Kate dangled the disc of her stethoscope so that Muriel could catch it in her hands. She smiled at the baby and got a big grin in response. For a moment she was completely distracted by the tiny fingers exploring the new toy.

Baby fingers were just *so* adorable...

These momentary distractions were becoming familiar now. She'd had nearly three weeks to get used to the idea of being pregnant herself. That, in the not-too-distant future, she would have one of these tiny people in her own life. Her own set of tiny little fingers and toes to marvel over. Her own smiles to make the world seem suddenly a much happier place.

Her own baby to hold and worry about and... and love...

She loved this baby growing inside her already.

She couldn't give her such an adult-sounding name, though. Her favourites were the classics, like Emily or Amy for a girl and James for a boy. Of course, James sounded a bit too grown-up, too, but he could be Jamie to start with, couldn't he?'

'Sorry?' Kate covered up that she hadn't heard Janet's question clearly by making a show of gently extracting her stethoscope from small fists and placing it on the tiny chest.

'I'm just wondering what I can do to keep her safe when we get home. I'm so scared that she's going to catch something else and I'll end up watching her on that breathing machine…' Janet's voice hitched '…not knowing if I was ever going to get to hold her again.'

'The best thing you can do is to keep her away as best you can from anyone who has any symptoms of a respiratory illness—even a cold. Don't let them hold her or kiss her. Don't let anyone smoke anywhere near her. And she'll be old enough for her vaccines soon. That's the best protection. Make sure all her caregivers are up to date with things like the whooping cough booster and flu shots.'

Kate was silent for a minute as she moved her stethoscope from one lung field to another. Muriel was staring up her with wide, blue eyes and one hand curled around the tubing of the stethoscope.

'That all sounds so much better... I think you're going to be able to go home very soon, sweetheart. Maybe tomorrow.'

Her next patient was a two-year-old boy who had suffered a serious leg fracture, requiring surgery, after an accident on a trampoline. Sean was a very different personality from the happy Muriel. Dark-haired and very shy, he was inclined to hide his face against his mother if spoken to directly by anyone he didn't know well. He'd been here long enough for Kate to become a familiar figure, though.

'Can you wiggle your toes for me, Sean? This little piggy goes to market...this little piggy stays home... Ooh... I saw that little piggy move. Yay!'

She shared a smile with Sean's mother. 'He's making great progress.'

'When can he go into a cast? And come home? My husband's about at the end of his tether with the older kids. My mum's great but she can't take much more time off work…'

'The surgeons are going to review him after his X-rays today. We should know something by this afternoon. I'll pop back and talk to you as soon as I can.'

Her registrar was shaking her head as they moved on. 'I don't know how some of these families cope. Did you know that Sean's the youngest of five and the oldest is only ten? How hard would that be?'

'I can't imagine.'

It was scary enough to think about being the caregiver for one tiny, defenceless baby and Kate was getting more worried about Georgia with every passing week. How would she cope on her own? Especially now that Luke was getting more excited about the possibility of a new life in New Zealand. He'd found several positions going, one in the biggest city of Auckland in the North Island and a couple in a much smaller town, at the top of the South Island, in a place called Nelson that seemed to have a hospital big enough to need specialist paediatric staff like both herself and Luke.

Last night, he'd shown her pictures of the kind of scenery they would have on their doorstep. Astonishingly beautiful beaches and forests and views of islands and it looked as if the sun shone all the time.

'Have you ever been to Nelson?' Kate asked her registrar.

'Only on holiday.'

'Was it sunny all the time?'

Her registrar laughed. 'Pretty much.'

'Would it be a good place to work?'

'It would be a dream. Great hospital with enough of a population base to keep things interesting. Not somewhere I can dream about until I get some impressive post-grad qualifications, though. It's competitive enough to give them the luxury of choosing the best.'

The comment came back to Kate as she finally finished her busy day and was struggling to open her umbrella as she emerged from the Eastern's front doors. She had arranged to meet Luke in a nearby pub across the main road for a quick meal before they went to an opening of a new art exhibition.

She would have to tell him about what she'd heard. That Nelson must be the place to pick if so many people wanted to live and work there. He wouldn't be fazed by hearing about how competitive it was to get a job. If anything, that would probably make him even keener. And he didn't need to worry, did he? Luke was the best in his field. And she had gathered some hard-won postgraduate qualifications herself. How good would it be if they could both get new job offers easily? A sign that it was the right thing to do?

Kate tilted her umbrella to try and stop it blowing inside out. She could feel her legs getting damp and cold as she hurried towards the controlled crossing at the intersection of these main roads and there was a knot in her stomach that she knew was caused by her worry about deserting Georgia. How could she be seriously considering emigrating?

Because this was the kind of weather she hated so much?

Because the dream of the perfect family deserved to have a perfect setting?

Maybe Georgia should consider the idea of emigrating herself? It wasn't as if she had family to help out here. How good would that be, to have her own baby growing up with her best friend's child as a kind of cousin? Georgia might actually like the idea. Not only would the father of her baby remain unknown, he could be half a world away and so much easier to forget.

Unless it had been one of the New Zealand paramedics that had been at the competition? That blond-headed guy they'd sat with at that first dinner maybe. What was his name...

Ken.

No... Dave.

He'd certainly been very friendly. He'd liked Georgia and he'd been a very long way from home. Why not throw a bit of casual sex into the enjoyment of a new experience?

Good grief…why hadn't that occurred to her before?

Slightly dazed, Kate realised that the lights had changed some time ago and most of the pedestrians waiting to cross were already more than halfway across the road.

And…wasn't that Luke standing on the corner outside the pub, waiting for her? She couldn't really tell from this distance but it seemed as if he was looking right at her, so she raised her hand in a wave. The unexpected pleasure of seeing him so soon prompted an automatic smile but it faded swiftly. Why wasn't he inside in the warmth? He didn't even have an umbrella, for heaven's sake…

The lights were flashing a warning now, but Kate made a run for it. Both she and Luke would only get a whole lot wetter if she waited for the next cycle of lights.

The rain was even heavier now and it distorted the headlights of the vehicles. Someone tooted and Kate turned her head for an instant, aware that she wasn't following the rules and probably deserved the reprimand.

That was why she didn't see the car in the next lane, hidden by the tooting SUV, taking off the instant the traffic lights changed.

She just saw the blur of headlights coming towards her.

And then…nothing…

CHAPTER EIGHT

No-o-o...

For just a heartbeat, Luke was frozen the spot with disbelief.

He'd seen Kate waiting at the corner for the lights to change and he'd wondered why it had taken her so long to follow the other pedestrians. She'd clearly been lost in thought so the contrast, when she'd spotted him, had been revealing.

Even from this distance, he could see how happy she had been to see him. That smile...

It had made him feel so...special. To be able to give someone pleasure simply by existing. By waiting to give them your company. He might be getting rather wet by standing outside like this but he wasn't cold. How could he be when such an astonishing warmth was being created inside him? And he wasn't going to go inside either. Not until Kate was here.

He was actually smiling himself as he saw her start to run across the road. He could see that the signal was flashing, which meant that you weren't supposed to start crossing at that point. He'd have to tease her about breaking rules like this. Except that she was breaking those rules because she wanted to be with *him* and Luke couldn't think of anybody else who had ever done that.

He heard the SUV toot its warning. And he saw the moment the car in the next lane took off, so fast its wheels skidded slightly on the wet road. Kate was running and, for a split second, it seemed that she was going to make it. It would be a near miss that would probably give her nothing more than a fright.

Except she didn't quite make it. He saw her falling. Saw her umbrella float away from her in a graceful arc, tumbling over itself before it hit the ground. More vehicles were sounding their horns now because few people could see why the traffic had stalled in front of a green light. The cacophony of sound seemed an appropriate background to the sense of panic that kicked in after Luke's momentary freeze.

Katy…

People were getting out of their vehicles by the time he sprinted into the middle of the road. Horns were still blaring and people were shouting.

'What the hell happened?'

'Call an ambulance.'

'The hospital's just down the road.'

'Call the police.'

Someone picked up Kate's umbrella and moved to hold it over the crumpled figure on the tarmac.

'I'm a doctor… Let me through…' Luke had to push past the gathering huddle of strangers. He dropped to his knees beside Kate, oblivious to the puddle he was kneeling in or the cold rain trickling down his face.

The light was flickering, with the shapes of people moving in front of headlights and the traffic lights changing, but he could see that Kate's eyes were closed.

Was she breathing?

Luke cradled the top of her head with his hand, not simply because he needed to stop any movement in case she had injured her neck, but because he needed to touch her for way more than medical reasons. He put his other hand gently on her abdomen. He'd be able to feel the movements of breathing more easily than see them in this light.

'Kate? Can you hear me?'

Luke could feel the muscles beneath his hand lurch as a deep breath was dragged in. And then Kate's eyelids flickered.

'Stay still, hon… Don't move…'

He heard the blast of a nearby siren.

'Move out of the way,' someone yelled.

A police car edged its way through the traffic that had now stopped in both directions. And behind that were the flashing beacons of an ambulance that had probably already been in the queue of traffic leaving the hospital.

Kate was blinking up at Luke now and her mouth opened. The distressed sound was only quiet but Luke would have heard it no matter how loud the background was. It cut through him like a knife.

'It's okay, Katy... Everything's going to be okay...'

Was it?

How badly was she hurt?

Maybe nothing was going to be okay. For either of them...

The fear that kicked in then was crippling. Unprofessional. It didn't matter that he could see that Kate was conscious and therefore had an open airway and was breathing. He needed to check for any major injuries. Blood loss...

It was just as well the paramedics were here now. Luke simply had to hold Kate's head still and he could lean close enough to try and give her reassurance.

Give himself reassurance, too?

'It's okay,' he kept repeating. 'Everything's going to be okay.'

'Did anyone see exactly what happened?' the paramedics asked. 'How fast was the car going? Was she knocked out?

'Yes,' Luke told them. 'She was unconscious when I got here.'

'Let's get a collar on and scoop her. We need to get her off the road.'

'No...' Kate was trying to move. 'I'm all right.'

'I think she fell,' someone spoke up from the huddle of onlookers. 'I'm not sure that the car actually touched her but it was a bit of a blur what with the rain and everything. It all happened so fast.'

'Stay still, Katy,' Luke said. 'We'll get you into A and E so we can check you out properly.' Right now, it didn't make a difference whether she had fallen or been hit by a car. She had hit her head hard enough to knock her unconscious and that could well indicate a serious injury.

A cervical collar was strapped around Kate's neck and the scoop stretcher that separated into two pieces to be eased in from either side of her body meant that she could be moved without interfering with the alignment of her spine. There were warm blankets to cover her with and the heating in the ambulance was turned up high but the trip back to the hospital only a block away was slowed because of the traffic jam and both Kate and Luke were shivering by the time they were under the bright lights of the emergency department.

'You're soaked,' Kate said. 'I'm s-so sorry, Luke. This was m-my fault…'

'Shh…it doesn't matter. Is anything hurting?'

'Let's get her onto the bed.' A consultant was waiting to lead the team in the resuscitation area Kate's stretcher was wheeled into. 'On my count. One, two…three…' The doctor's eyes widened as he looked down at his patient. *'Kate?'*

'Car versus pedestrian,' the paramedic said. 'She was KO'd.'

'It was my fault,' Kate whispered. 'The lights were changing and I made a run for it.'

The scoop stretcher was being unclipped and removed. The consultant was keeping Kate's head still.

'Any trouble breathing?'

'No.'

'Any pain?'

People were removing Kate's clothing. Some-one was sticking ECG electrodes to her skin.

'I... No, I don't think so. Maybe my head, a bit...'

Her hair was wet, dark against the white sheet on the bed. To his horror, Luke could see a faint pink stain appearing.

'She's bleeding,' he snapped. 'From a head in-jury.'

The consultant glanced up. 'And you are...?

'Luke Anderson. I'm Kate's...' The hesitation was involuntary. What could he say?

I'm Kate's friend?

I'm the father of Kate's baby?

He was much more than either of those things, though, wasn't he?

He was Kate's *person*.

The person who loved her enough to want to spend the rest of his life with her.

So much so that in that awful moment of standing there, frozen, on the side of the road, he'd known that he couldn't live without her.

He was…oh, God…he was *in love* with her, wasn't he?

And it felt like he always had been. The truth of it had just been hiding but something had shifted in the shock of seeing Kate hit by that car and now wave after wave of this extraordinary feeling was washing over him, threatening to knock him off his feet.

'Luke's a surgeon.' Kate was filling the gap his hesitation had left. 'Over at Edinburgh's Royal Children's Hospital. And he's…he's my fiancé.'

Fiancé?

But Kate had brushed off the idea of a registry office wedding as being unnecessary. Undesirable, even. On top of his stunning epiphany, the ground was still moving beneath his feet. What on earth was going on here?

'No way…' one of the nurses in the room gasped, looking up from her task of wrapping a blood-pressure cuff around an arm. 'You kept that quiet, Kate.'

'Let's celebrate the engagement later, shall we?' But the consultant was smiling. 'Right now, I want to see what damage you've done to yourself. What's the BP?'

'Ninety-five over sixty.'

'I'm usually on the low side.' Kate's voice sounded steadier now. 'Look… I can wiggle my fingers and toes. Nothing hurts.'

'We'll get an X-ray of your C-spine before we take that collar off. You hit your head hard enough to get knocked out, even if it wasn't for long. And I don't like the look of that bruise on your hip. Could have been where the car clipped you. We should check for a pelvic fracture, too.'

'No…no X-rays…'

Another tiny, surprised silence fell.

'I'm…' Kate's glance locked with Luke's, her eyes dark with something that looked like fear. 'I'm pregnant.'

The fear was contagious. Maybe he was less anxious about Kate now that he could see how alert she was and that she was claiming to feel all right, but there was someone else to worry about, too, wasn't there?

He took hold of her hand and squeezed it. Kate squeezed back but didn't release the pressure. She was clinging to his hand and that was fine by him. He didn't want her to let go. The pressure felt like an anchor, holding him steady in a space where he still felt like he was spinning out of control.

He had fallen in love with her. The one thing he had sworn never to do. The one thing that he couldn't trust. And Kate felt the same way. She'd said it herself only days ago. That she wasn't in love with him. That that was the only reason that the pact was working out so perfectly. He could hear very clear echoes of her voice.

If that changed, it wouldn't work, would it?'

You've persuaded me to buy into the pact and give up on my lifelong dream of being swept off my feet by a grand passion...

'Right.' The consultant had taken the new information in his stride. 'Let's do a thorough secondary survey, then. We'll hold off on the X-rays

until we know what we're dealing with. Now…
let's have a good look at your head. What day
is it today, Kate?'

'Wednesday.'

'Time?'

'Um…it was after five when I left work. I was
running late to meet Luke at the pub. Ow…!'

'Sore?'

'Bit tender.'

'You've got a good lump. And it's grazed a
bit but I can't feel anything boggy. I don't think
you've fractured your skull.'

'The bruising's superficial,' a registrar added.
'More consistent with hitting the road than contact with a vehicle. Abdo's soft. Pelvis is stable.'

'I think I tripped,' Kate said. 'I remember seeing the lights of the car really close and thinking
that I had to get out of the way.'

The consultant undid the straps of the neck collar. 'Don't move yet.' He was palpating the back
of her neck. 'Any pain?'

'No.'

'Try moving your neck very gently. Chin down…and up…'

'It's fine, honestly.'

'To the right…and left… No pain?'

'None. I've just got a bit of a headache. It's nothing that a paracetamol won't fix. Can I sit up now? Please?'

She was still holding Luke's hand as pillows were found and she was helped to sit up a short time later, when everyone was satisfied that she hadn't suffered a serious injury.

That was how he could feel her wince.

'What is it? What's hurting?'

'It's nothing.' But Kate's hand had gone to her abdomen. 'Just a bit of a cramp.'

She looked up in time to catch the swift glance between Luke and the consultant. 'What? It wasn't enough of a bump to have hurt the baby…' Her voice wobbled. 'Was it…?'

'Let's do an ultrasound. How many weeks are you, Kate?'

'We only found out a few weeks ago. Around seven weeks, I guess.'

'Try not to worry. Let's move you out of Resus to somewhere a bit quieter. We'll do the ultrasound. I want you to stay under observation for a bit, anyway, to make sure it's only a mild concussion.' He smiled at Kate as they prepared to move her bed. 'You've been lucky, haven't you?'

Lucky?

Kate didn't bother trying to wipe away the tears rolling down her face. She didn't open her eyes either.

'It could have been worse.' Luke's voice sounded raw. 'You could have been killed, Katy.'

She started to nod but it made her headache worse. Instead, she dragged her hand over her face, taking a deep breath that went in as a sniff and came out as a sigh.

'It's okay, Luke. You don't have to stay here all night.'

'I'm not going anywhere.'

With an effort, Kate opened her eyes. 'Don't be daft. Your clothes are still damp. My grandma would have said you'll catch your death if you sit around like that.'

'Urban myth. Like breakfast being the most important meal of the day.'

'Which is another thing. When did you last have something to eat?'

'I can't remember. Probably about the same time you did.'

The lopsided tilt of Luke's mouth showed his appreciation of her attempt to show concern for his well-being but was that really what she was trying to do?

Maybe she needed him to go away and leave her alone to deal with this.

Because it was huge.

Heartbreaking…

'I'm okay, Luke.' Kate swallowed hard. She needed him to believe that. Just like she needed him to believe that she wasn't in love with him. If he knew just how badly she needed him to hold her right now and keep telling her that everything would be okay—like he had when she'd been lying on that road—he might guess how she really felt.

How afraid she was of losing him, as well as their baby.

Was the perfect pact starting to unravel?

'It's not as if it was...*real.*' Kate had to squeeze her eyes shut. Her last word came out as no more than a whisper.

'What do you mean?' Luke sounded bewildered. 'Of course it was real.'

He was right. The baby had been very real. Knowing they were going to be parents had been very real. They'd been scouring the globe for the perfect place to raise a family, for heaven's sake.

She had loved this baby already...

Maybe what she was actually saying was that their partnership wasn't real? That there was something clinical about implementing that pact? That she didn't think that Luke could feel this loss as much as her because he wasn't as invested as she was in either the relationship or their future family?

But when the silence had continued long enough to make her open her eyes, what she could see in Luke's face was confusing. He looked so tired.

Sad…

As if he was hurting as much as she was?

It wasn't really fair to think she was the only one to feel devastated by this unexpected turn of events. He'd been delighted that she'd become pregnant so easily. As if it was confirmation that they were doing the right thing by basing their entire future on what was, as far as Luke was concerned, a kind of arranged marriage.

Or was it something else that was bothering him so much?

A flash of fear cut through her own grief. Was Luke realising that they couldn't control everything by being so pragmatic about how they made their choices? That maybe the pact wasn't worth the metaphorical paper it had been written on?

'I just meant that it was so early,' she said quietly. 'There's always a risk in the first trimester. And it happened so much faster than we expected, too. We'd hardly had time to get used to the idea, had we?'

'Mmm.' Luke didn't sound convinced. His gaze was searching. 'Are you sure you're okay, Katy?

With the biggest effort ever, Kate summoned a smile. 'I will be. I've got a thumping headache and all I want to do is sleep for a bit.'

'You'll stay here until they're happy to let you go, though?'

'Yeah…'

'And you can't be at home by yourself. You'll need someone who can spot any signs of a change in the signs or symptoms of a head injury.'

'Georgie's more than capable. She's coming in later with some clean clothes for me and she said that she's juggled her shifts so that she can stay home tomorrow.'

Kate didn't add that it hadn't been a problem because Georgia had confessed her pregnancy at work and was restricted to lighter duties now. She didn't want to think about how obvious Georgia's bump had become in the last few weeks.

The kind of bump that Kate was no longer going to experience in the near future.

More tears were not far away. That she wanted Luke to stay so badly was a warning sign that things could unravel even more than they had already. If she wanted to keep at least their relationship intact, he needed to go. Now.

'Go home, Luke. I just want to go to sleep for a bit so there's no point in you sitting here.'

'But…' Luke had an odd expression on his face. As if he was debating whether or not to say something that she might not want to hear.

She could help him decide. Make it clear that she *didn't* want to hear it.

'Go. Please.' Kate closed her eyes again to signal an end to the conversation. 'I'll call you tomorrow.'

'Are you sure you're up to this?'

Kate didn't pause in her progress up the steep hill. 'Stop trying to wrap me in cotton wool, Luke. I'm fine.'

'No headache today?'

'I haven't had a headache in more than a week. I'm fine. It was a mild concussion and it was nearly two weeks ago. I only needed a day or two off work and this is the first day off that we've both had since then.' Kate's smile was bright.

'Normal service has resumed. And I'm really looking forward to finally getting to see the inside of Edinburgh Castle.'

'Me, too.' But Luke could feel himself frowning as he stared straight ahead. It didn't feel as if 'normal service' had been resumed. There had been something different about Kate ever since the devastating news about the baby.

Something that seemed…off-key.

He'd tried to talk to her about it, more than once, but she'd brushed it off as being no big deal.

It was all too easy and perfect anyway, she'd said. *Fairy-tales don't happen in real life. We both know that.*

And that had been that, apparently. She had thrown herself back into work as soon as she'd been given the all-clear from her concussion and bruising and she seemed to be coping perfectly well.

Too well?

Like the way she'd agreed to this outing today, to visit Edinburgh Castle, as a fabulous idea—something she'd been intending to do for ages.

Her smile had been bright when they'd met at the bottom of the hill and the quick hug and kiss on the cheek had told him how pleased she was to see him.

It was Kate who was keeping the conversation going, too, every time a silence fell.

Like it had in the last couple of minutes.

'Oh, look at that. Another specialist whisky shop.'

'It's a popular drop in these parts. There's a kilt-maker. Do you want to go and try one on?'

Kate laughed. 'No, thanks. Do you?'

Luke grinned. 'I'd be too worried about a windy day, wearing one of those.' He resisted another urge to take hold of her hand as they kept climbing towards the iconic castle on the top of the hill.

He hadn't held her hand since that awful night in the emergency department.

They hadn't made love since then either.

And it was killing him that Kate didn't seem bothered. That it felt as if she had taken a step back. Because the intimacy that had been created by knowing that they had a baby on the way had been extinguished?

He wanted to tell her that they could try again. That, this time, everything would be all right.

But he couldn't make promises like that, could he? She was right. Fairy-tales rarely happened in real life. Look at the mess his marriage to Nadia had turned into. Not believing in fairy-tales had been the very reason he'd decided that resurrecting 'the pact' had been such a brilliant idea and that it had a much better chance of working long term.

And it had worked.

Until the moment he'd realised that he was in love with Kate.

That should have been enough to make him back off. To—figuratively—tear up that pact because it was no longer valid.

He could never be simply her friend any more.

But the last thing Luke wanted to do was back off. He couldn't, even if it meant he was headed for the same kind of heartbreak that he'd experienced before. He was too far gone.

He wanted the fairy-tale, dammit.

All the 'crazy stuff' as he'd called it back when he'd had that conversation with Kate on their first dinner date. When he'd set out to persuade her that friendship was the way to go. That the pact had merit.

How ironic was that?

She'd accepted the invitation and now she was the one who thought that it could only work if the ground rules were respected. And *he* was the one who wanted more. Who wanted the crazy stuff of not being able to keep their hands off each other. Of drowning in eye contact that felt like you'd discovered the meaning of life. That kind of telepathy where you could say so much through no more than a touch or a glance.

Could it happen one day? If they could stay together and build on what they already had?

If it didn't, could he live with that? Being in love with someone who didn't feel the same way about him?

He didn't really have a choice. Not if he didn't want to risk losing her.

He'd lapsed into silence again and the quick glance from Kate told him that it had gone on for a heartbeat too long.

'I haven't even talked to you properly for a few days,' she said. 'How's work been?'

'Busy. Had a hell of case yesterday. A ten-year-old kid who had a DVD in his hand when the car crashed. It sliced his neck like a knife and nicked his carotid artery.'

'Good grief. He could have bled to death in no time at all.'

'I know. The ambulance crew did a brilliant job. Didn't Georgia tell you about it? She was on the crew.'

'I've barely seen her in the last couple of days. Sometimes our hours make us like ships passing in the night. I worked late last night so she was in bed by the time I got home and I slept in this morning, with it being my first day off for a while, so she was gone by the time I got up.' Kate raised her eyebrows. 'I thought she was on lighter duties now. What was she doing out on the road?'

'I asked her about that. She's been given one of those cars apparently. The ones that get sent out first—or as backup for a major incident? It means she can assess a scene for what's needed and give urgent treatment but has to call for backup for any lifting or transfer.'

'Oh, yeah.' Kate was smiling again. 'She told me that was in the pipeline a while back. I got the impression she had been whinging so much about the prospect of being stuck in an office and bored stiff, they bowed under pressure.'

The smile seemed to fade more quickly than it usually did. It had to be hard for Kate to be living with someone who was so far along in her pregnancy that it was the first thing everyone noticed about her. It had given Luke a jolt when he'd seen Georgia yesterday. Just for a split second, before he'd focused on the critically injured young boy being brought into his care, he'd felt the loss all over again.

The loss of their baby. *His* baby. The start of the family he wanted to have with Kate.

That wasn't what Kate wanted to talk about

right now, though. And if he steered the conversation in that direction, this easy communication between them would dry up completely because Kate probably wouldn't make the effort to break that silence.

'She certainly got a good dose of excitement this time.' Luke abandoned any desire to change the direction of their conversation. 'She came back in the helicopter with the boy and got someone else to take her car back, I guess. Anyway, she was keeping pressure on the bleed and she wasn't going to let go of the padding until he was in Theatre, if necessary.'

'And was it?'

'He was in decompensating hypovolaemic shock. I wasn't going to risk her letting go and getting any further blood loss until we could stabilise him. We started fluid resuscitation in Emergency and then I put a clamp on the artery the instant Georgia let go, and we rushed him up to Theatre as fast as possible. All very dramatic—it was like we were in an episode of some TV medical show.'

Talking shop was the last thing Luke wanted to be doing right now but at least Kate seemed genuinely interested. More engaged than she had been, in fact, ever since the accident.

'Georgia wanted to watch so I let her gown up and come into Theatre with us.'

'She must have been thrilled. I'm sure I'll hear all about it when I get home tonight. If we're not too late with our dinner, that is.'

Luke's heart sank. Did that mean Kate had no intention of coming back to his apartment this evening?

No desire to share his bed, even for an hour or two?

He'd done his research. He knew that it was safe to have sex again as soon as you and your partner felt physically and emotionally ready but that it was best to wait until any miscarriage-related bleeding had stopped. That usually happened within two weeks.

Kate had said that 'normal service' had resumed but she wouldn't refer to making love in such pragmatic terms, would she?

His heart sank even further.

Why not?

It wasn't 'making love' as far as she was concerned, was it? It was just an unexpectedly good physical connection.

A friendship…with benefits.

Had he really believed he'd found the answer when he'd been so blown away by how amazing the sex had been with Kate? That a friendship with benefits was nothing short of perfect?

This didn't feel perfect any more.

It felt…wrong…

CHAPTER NINE

IT WASN'T WORKING.

The amount of effort Kate was putting into making things feel the way they had before didn't seem to be making any real difference.

Here they were, on a day out to explore something interesting, and it was nothing like any time they had spent together in the last few months—like that day when they'd hired bicycles and gone down the disused railway lines or that memorable, misty day when they'd gone to hunt for the Loch Ness monster. That easy enjoyment of each other's company was missing.

This felt…awkward?

It should be enjoyable. Being inside the towering stone walls of the iconic castle she had admired for so long had been fascinating from the moment they'd walked beneath the massive portcullis gate with its spikes raised to allow visitors to enter. There'd been museums to visit, steep stairs to climb and cobbled streets to wander down. The ancient chapel of St Margaret's had been beautiful and the poignant dog's cemetery where soldiers had buried their beloved canine companions had almost brought her to tears. The silence between them at that point had gone on even longer than any of the previous ones and, embarrassingly, they'd both tried to break it at the same time, with some comment intended to break an increasingly tense atmosphere.

It should have been an opportunity to share a smile. To talk about what was creating this new distance between them and do something about fixing it.

But Kate had hesitated and the moment had been lost.

Because she was wondering if Luke might not actually want to fix it?

There'd been a brief period when Kate had thought they had been finding some old ground, when they'd been talking about the trauma case

Luke and Georgia had been involved with yesterday, but as soon as the conversation had tailed off, she'd realised it was the sort of communication she would have with any of her medical colleagues.

It had lacked that extra dimension that talking to Luke usually had. The feeling that she could sense what he wasn't saying. He must have been deeply concerned to have a child presented to him with a life-threatening neck injury. Kate would have found the prospect terrifying but, thinking back on the conversation, she realised that Luke had sounded calm. Almost bored? As if he didn't really want to be talking about it but was making an effort to be polite.

'What does the guide say about these cannons?'

'Um…' Luke scanned the pamphlet he'd picked up in the visitor's centre. 'It's the Argyle Battery. They date back to the Napoleonic wars with France.'

'Wow…' Kate eyed the impressive weapons.

She was trying to be cheerful. To reassure Luke that she was over the trauma of her accident and losing the baby. That she was still on board with their plans for the future.

That 'the pact' was still valid.

But something had changed between them. Something that was big enough to be convincing her that maybe Luke had changed his mind but he couldn't think of a way to broach the subject yet.

Not all relationships ended with some kind of spectacular break-up, did they? Sometimes they just fizzled out slowly as the distance between people got larger and larger.

Kate didn't want that to happen to her and Luke.

The prospect of losing him was frightening. Life would never be the same without the company of the man she was so sure was her soul mate.

But doubts were creeping in now. This didn't feel as if she was in the company of the one person she couldn't imagine living without.

He hadn't even kissed her since the night of

the accident. Not in any way that was on a level other than mere friendship.

Wandering around the perimeter of the castle, with its irregular outline, they came across an odd, three-sided corner. A space that felt disconnected from the traffic of other tourists. For a long time they both stared out at the astonishing view, from what looked like most of the city of Edinburgh and much further—to hills and snow-capped mountains and the sea.

It was Luke who broke this silence, with a heartfelt sigh.

'Makes you think, doesn't it?' He turned his head to catch Kate's gaze. 'I wonder how many people have stood in this spot and looked out at that view and tried to figure out what life is all about. Or what *they* really want from it.'

Was that what Luke was thinking about?

Kate's heart skipped a beat. If she hesitated this time, she might not get another opportunity. Despite her determination, her voice sounded small and quiet against the backdrop of those limitless horizons.

'What do *you* want, Luke?'

He was silent for so long she thought he wasn't going to answer. When he did, he spoke slowly and his voice was almost sombre.

'I guess I want to grab life with both hands and make the most of it. To have someone to do that with. Someone who feels the same way about the important things...'

Kate's throat felt tight.

'We can do that.'

'What?' Luke's quick sideways glance was puzzled.

'Grab life. Together. A new life...'

His eyebrows rose further. 'You mean in New Zealand?'

'Why not? Have you applied for that job in Nelson yet?'

'No. I wouldn't do that without talking to you about it. And I wasn't sure you still wanted to.'

'Why not?' Kate's mouth felt dry now. She'd been right—he had been rethinking things. Making assumptions about how she felt?

'It had been all about raising a family. I thought

you might have changed your mind after... after...'

'Losing the baby?' Kate didn't try and blink back the tears that pricked her eyes. 'You know what?'

'What?'

'I know I said that it wasn't real because it had been so early in the pregnancy but...it was *so* real for me. It was silly but I already loved that baby. I already *felt* like a mother. And I knew... I knew how much I wanted it to be real.'

'Oh, *Katy*...' Luke's arms were around her. Holding her tight. 'It *was* real. It was real from the moment we found out. I felt like a father. I told you I was thrilled. And I was.' She felt the shuddering breath he took in. 'When I left you in the hospital that night and went home, I cried.'

Kate kept her head buried against his shoulder, aware of his warmth and the faint thud of his heartbeat. She soaked in the smell of his worn, leather jacket. The smell of Luke...

She shouldn't have sent him home that night. It hadn't been only her who had lost something important, had it? They should have cried together. But she'd been so afraid of that kind of intimacy pushing him away because it might have revealed just how much in love with him she was.

Even now, in his arms like this, an alarm bell was sounding, snippets of an imaginary conversation flashing into her brain.

The horror in Luke's voice. *You're in love with me?*

I'm sorry... I know I've broken the rules...

I'm sorry too, Kate. This has ruined everything...

She took a deep breath, shutting out the unwanted voices.

'I thought you were crazy, you know?'

'Why?'

'Your idea that nothing more than friendship was enough to make the kind of relationship that could last for ever. I believe you now, though.'

She could feel a sudden tension in the arms around her but Luke's words were steady. 'So you don't still believe that being in love is important?'

She couldn't look up at him. Not yet.

'What we have is better. The best. I... I wouldn't want anything else.'

As she felt the tension ebb, she could finally look up. Find a tentative smile, although that wobbled when she saw the way Luke was looking at her.

That *tenderness*...

She could believe that he loved her as much as it was possible to love someone. That he was *in love* with her, even if he didn't realise it.

And it was enough. Surely it would always be enough.

She found herself rising up on tiptoe. Lifting her face in an invitation to be kissed. An invitation that Luke didn't hesitate to accept.

The kiss was just as tender as that look had been. Enough to bring another prickle of tears to Kate's eyes, but these weren't sad tears.

They were tears of relief.

Everything was going to be all right.

This time, when they carried on their tour of the castle, they did it hand in hand.

'Do you really want me to apply for that job in Nelson?'

'If you want to. I'll start looking for something for me, too.'

'It's a long way away. It's the other side of the world, you know. About as far away from here as it's possible to get.'

'I know.' But Luke would be there and that was all Kate would need.

'You'd be leaving your friends behind. Like Georgia.'

'Yeah… I was worried about that but then it occurred to me that she might want to emigrate too.'

'Really?'

'Don't let on that I've told you, but I've got the suspicion that the mystery father of her baby might be a Kiwi paramedic that she met. I know that she's determined to be a single parent but I don't really believe that she doesn't want more than that. And who knows? Maybe she would rethink things—especially if she was in the same country as her baby's father.'

'Interesting idea.' But Luke seemed distracted.

'Does it make it harder for you? Being around her at the moment? It made me think about things when I saw her yesterday.'

'The baby, you mean?' Kate nodded slowly. 'Yes. It's hard.'

'Do you want to try again? Or is it too soon?'

'I… Yes… I do want to try again. Maybe not just yet, though.'

Luke mirrored her nod. Their tour of the castle was almost done and the rift between them seemed to have narrowed to almost nothing. Maybe they would go and find a cosy restaurant soon. She could drink some wine again now and things would become even more relaxed.

They weren't that far from Luke's apartment.

If they went back there and made love, she'd know that things were really back to normal. That she could trust they'd overcome the first, palpable obstacle in their relationship.

But as the castle walls towered higher behind them as they started walking down the hill again, Luke cleared his throat. 'There's something else…'

'Oh?' Kate's steps slowed.

'That night when you had the accident and we were in the emergency department and that consultant wanted to know who I was, you said I was your fiancé.'

Kate had stopped now. Or maybe it was Luke who had paused, waiting for her response. The traffic of other people flowed around them but there was only one person who mattered at the moment.

'It seemed like the easiest way to explain things.'

'I know. But… I liked it.'

'Oh…' Someone bumped Kate's shoulder but she barely noticed.

'I know you said we didn't need a wedding or the piece of paper but…you might think it's silly but I think I *do* want it.'

'It's not silly.' No more than feeling like parents when the reality was still a long way in the future.

'So you'd do that? Marry me?'

It might not be any more romantic than the first time he'd proposed to her and it was rather public but nobody else in this busy street had any idea of how private this conversation was. And she couldn't complain about the setting when it had the backdrop of this beautiful, ancient castle.

'When?'

'Soon. I knew there was a good reason to do that paperwork. If I can find a registry office with a space, we could do it tomorrow.'

Kate's jaw dropped. 'You're kidding. I don't even have a *dress*.'

'Okay…next week, then?' Luke was grinning as he pulled her into his arms again. 'The clothes don't matter, Katy. It's what we do with the rest of our lives that matters and… I want to do it with you. I love you.'

'Are you free Thursday afternoon?'

'I'm not sure. Why?' Georgia had opened the fridge and was staring inside. 'I'm hungry but I have no idea what I want to eat.'

'Stay away from the eggs.'

'I'm over that now.' With a sigh, she pushed

the door closed. 'But there's nothing in there that looks interesting. Let's go out for a curry.'

'Do you really think that's a good idea? Anyway, I'm making a great salad here.'

Georgia glanced at the chopping board in front of Kate and grimaced. 'I'm hungry. Salad isn't real food. And I'm bored. Let's go down Buchanan Street and do some late night shopping and then find something exciting to eat. What about nachos? You *love* nachos.'

'Mmm. I can't deny that.'

'And shopping is always fun. We haven't done that for ages.'

'I guess you do need some maternity clothes.' Kate paused in her task of slicing a capsicum and eyed her friend's midriff. 'You know, you look a lot bigger than I would have expected for not quite five months along.'

She turned to give Georgia her full attention. 'Is there something you're not telling me? Like, that you were already pregnant when we went off to that competition? Was it just a cover story that you were planning to hook up with someone you'd never have to see again?'

Georgia shook her head. 'But yeah…there is something I haven't told you.'

'Uh-oh…'

'It's not something bad. I didn't tell you to start with because I knew you'd worry more. And then, after your accident, I didn't want to make things worse…'

'How could it have made things any worse?'

Georgia closed her eyes. 'It's twins.'

The knife clattered onto the bench. Stunned, Kate walked to the table and sat down. Georgia followed her example.

'I'm sorry. It's like adding insult to injury, isn't it? I know you were excited about being pregnant, too.'

'It's not that.' Kate summoned a smile. 'I'm okay, really. Luke and I are going to try again as soon as we're ready.' She rubbed at her forehead with her fingers. 'It's… Oh, my God, Georgie… how are you going to cope with *two* babies on your own?'

'I'll cope.'

'But if Luke gets this job in New Zealand, I might be out of the country by the time the babies are born. You don't have any family to help.' She bit her bottom lip. 'I'll tell him I can't go until you're settled. Or…you'll just have to emigrate too.'

'I told you I don't want to move to New Zealand. I'm Scottish. This is my home. I'll come and visit, though. Hey…you're not going to *cry*, are you? I'm happy about this.'

'You are?'

'Of course. I'm getting an instant family. I won't have to go hunting for another father down the track so that my kid isn't an only child, like us.'

'But…' Kate's breath came out in a whoosh. 'You'll have to get two of everything. It'll be more expensive. Harder. You won't get any sleep. This makes everything so much *bigger*…'

'Including my waistline.' Georgia grinned but then sighed. 'This is why I didn't want to tell you, Kate. I knew you'd start worrying about everything and this is *my* business. *My* choice. I'll cope. One step at a time. And I don't want you to tell anybody. You have to promise not to say anything. Even to Luke.'

'Why?'

'Because I want to keep working as long as I can. You know how word gets around in medical circles. If other people react like you and just see the problems, I might find I don't even have light duties available any more. And then I won't be able to save enough money and things really will be harder.'

Kate was silent. Was that really what she was doing—only seeing the problems? Georgia was genuinely happy about this and she should be supporting her best friend.

'And I don't want you changing any of your plans because of me. I'll miss you like crazy, of course, but I think it's brilliant that you're going to go and have an exciting new life in New Zealand. You and Luke belong together. You're perfect for each other. Has he asked you to marry him yet?'

'Yes.'

Georgia gasped. 'And you didn't *tell* me? That's *way* worse than me not telling you I've got two bairns on board.'

'I was about to tell you. That's why I asked whether you were free on Thursday afternoon. At two o'clock? I…um…need a bridesmaid.'

'And you're telling me this now? With…one, two…' Georgia was counting on her fingers. 'With *three* days to go?'

'I only just found out a couple of hours ago. We weren't planning on doing it this fast, but there was a cancellation at the registry office in Edinburgh and if we hadn't grabbed it, we might have had to wait for months. It's no big deal, Georgie.'

Georgia was shaking her head. 'I can't believe this. Me? I could imagine ducking into a registry office or running off to Gretna Green for a quickie marriage if I had the inclination to marry anybody, which I *don't*, but you? I always thought you'd go for the whole meringue dress and rose petal confetti and some mushy love song echoing around the church as you walked down the aisle.'

Kate shrugged. 'The window dressing isn't what's important.'

'It is to some people.'

'I love Luke. He loves me.'

'He actually said the "L" word?'

Kate nodded, a soft smile curving her lips. He *had* said it. And even if he'd only meant it in the spirit of deep friendship, that look in his eyes had told her everything she'd needed to know.

That this was real.

That it could last a lifetime.

It didn't matter that he wasn't *in* love with her. Or that this wedding was merely a formality.

It *didn't* matter. So why did it feel like her smile was fading into oblivion?

'Wow…'

'I know, right?'

'And you're happy?'

Kate's nod was firm. Was she trying to convince Georgia or herself? 'So happy.'

'That makes two of us, then.' Georgia was smiling now. 'But this lack of window dressing business, that doesn't apply to *you*, does it?'

'How do you mean?'

'You're going to wear a dress? Get your hair done? Carry some flowers?'

'Yeah…of course. I want it to be special.'

'So what are you going to wear?'

'I don't know. I haven't had time to think about it yet.

'It has to be new.'

'Does it?'

'Of course it does. This is the start of the rest of your life. And there'll be photographs. And… good grief… *I'm* going to be in those photographs. I've got to find a dress that doesn't make me look like a sack of potatoes.' Georgia grabbed the corner of the table to help her get to her feet. 'Come on. We're going shopping.'

'What do you think?'

Kate stared at her reflection as Georgia stood back, hair-straighteners still in her hand.

The soft, shiny curls of her blonde hair brushed her shoulders. Her make-up was better than anything she would have achieved herself. She was wearing the pretty dress they had found the other evening—a lace over silk number that was a shade of blue darker than her eye colour.

With the simple bunch of daisies waiting downstairs for her, her look would be complete—and perfect for an understated registry office wedding.

Their timing was perfect, too. They'd both managed to leave work in time to get ready at home and they still had almost thirty minutes to drive to Edinburgh and find a parking space in the central city. It was getting tight but, even if parking was difficult, they wouldn't be more than a few minutes late and that was traditional for brides, wasn't it?

This was it.

Her wedding day.

Kate met Georgia's gaze in the mirror.

'I can't do it.'

Georgia grinned. 'Uh-oh…pre-wedding nerves. I'll get you a glass of wine or something.'

The new curls tickled her neck as Kate shook her head slowly.

'No. Wine won't make any difference. This isn't nerves. I just can't do it.'

'What…you don't want to marry Luke any more?'

Kate shook her head again. 'It's not that either. I *do* want to marry Luke. More than anything. But I can't do it like this.'

'Like what? You mean the registry office thing?' Georgie pulled the plug from the wall but kept the hair-straighteners in her hand as she sank onto the side of Kate's bed. 'I was right. You want the meringue dress and rose petals.'

Kate was beginning to feel like a puppet, repeating her headshake yet again. Her limbs felt heavy as well—as if she wouldn't be able to move unless someone pulled the right strings.

'I can't marry someone I'm deceiving like this.'

Georgia glanced at her watch, biting her bottom lip. 'So…what do you want to do? Just not show up?'

And jilt the man she loved?

'No, of course not.'

'You want to text Luke and tell him you're not coming?'

'I can't do something like that in a text message.'

'Phone him?'

'I don't know.' Kate pressed a hand to her mouth. 'I don't know what to do, Georgie. I just know that this feels wrong.'

'Okay.' Georgia got to her feet with the kind of calm that only someone used to dealing with emergency situations could display. 'Here's what we'll do. We'll get in the car and drive to Edinburgh. You can talk to me on the way. If you still feel the same way when we get there, you can ring Luke. Or talk to him face to face.'

Face to face.

Yes…that would be the brave thing to do. The honest thing.

And Luke deserved her honesty at the very least.

It was good that Georgia was pulling her strings. Kate got to her feet and went downstairs. She walked past the bunch of daisies and headed for the car. She heard the door slam behind her and then Georgia got into the driver's seat. She handed Kate the bunch of daisies.

'Just in case,' she murmured. Once out of the driveway, she put her foot down.

'We haven't got a siren on,' Kate said. 'Take it easy.'

'Sorry…' Georgia slowed the car a little. 'It's the tension.'

'No… I'm sorry. I shouldn't have let it get to this. But I didn't know how important it would suddenly seem. I've been living a lie.' It was all becoming clear in her head as the words started tumbling out. 'It was so important to Luke that our relationship be based on that stupid pact. That we would both be very clear about exactly how we felt about each other because we wouldn't be blinded by being in love. And I've let him believe that I was in the same place. I pretty much promised him that I hadn't fallen in love with him.'

'Maybe he won't mind,' Georgia said. 'He *loves* you. He told you that he loves you.'

'Yes, but not like that. It's like when I tell you that I love *you*.'

'You haven't told me that in a long time.' Georgia turned her head to smile at Kate. 'Do you love me?'

'Of course I do. But I'm not *in* love with you.'

'Thank goodness for that. We've got enough complications.' But Georgia was still smiling as she negotiated a turn that would take them towards the registry office. 'I love you, too.'

They drove in silence after that. The traffic was heavy and it was taking longer than it should. They were going to be late.

'Oh, *look*…there's a parking space. Almost right outside the registry office. It's a miracle.'

A minute later and they were parked. The engine of the car had been turned off. And Georgia was waiting quietly.

'So, what now? Do you want to ring Luke? Or go and find him and talk to him?'

Kate's heart was hammering. Her phone was shaking in her hand. 'I can't ring. But if I go in there, he'll think I've come to marry him. Walking in there and saying I can't do it is almost as bad as not turning up at all.'

What if she walked in there and saw him waiting for her? Would he be looking impossibly gorgeous in a suit and tie, despite what he'd said about clothes being unimportant? He'd be smiling, wouldn't he? Maybe looking at her the way he had when he'd been holding her in his arms up there in the castle whose walls dominated the top of the road they were parked on.

In the face of that kind of tenderness, hope even, she might well lose the courage she was summoning to be honest.

Georgia looked at her watch. 'It's nearly a quarter past two. We have to do something.' She drummed her fingers on the steering wheel. 'How 'bout *I* go in? That way he'll have a warning that something's up. And I can tell him that you need to talk to him. And then I'll show him where we're parked and stay out of your way for a while.'

She didn't wait for Kate's response. She was already easing her expanding belly past the steering wheel and out of the car.

Kate watched her disappear up the steps that led into the building further up the street.

And then she waited.

She closed her eyes and tried not to think of the expression that might be on Luke's face when he came to get into the car and talk to her.

How disappointed he was going to be when she told him the truth.

But she was doing the right thing.

Luke trusted her enough to be prepared to make a public commitment to spend the rest of his life with her. Maybe—and this was a glimmer of hope she couldn't quite extinguish—Georgia was right and he wouldn't mind. He might even laugh off the idea that she'd fallen in love with him and tell her that she'd get over it one day. He might actually want to go through with the ceremony but he deserved the option of changing his mind.

Kate couldn't change hers. She would never get over being in love with him.

Minutes ticked past as her thoughts whirled and settled, getting a little more despondent with each circuit. She was holding the bunch of daisies in her hand so tightly they seemed to be wilting right before her eyes.

Like her dreams of the future…?

With her eyes downcast, focussed on the flowers, she didn't see the person approaching the car. The door being wrenched opened made her jump.

And then her heart sank like a stone.

'What happened? He…he doesn't even want to *talk* to me?'

Georgia shook her head. 'He's not there, Kate.'

'What? He didn't even wait for fifteen minutes…?'

Georgia shook her head again. 'It's not that.' She reached out to touch Kate's hand. 'I'm sorry…but apparently he didn't turn up at all.'

CHAPTER TEN

'WHAT ARE YOU DOING?'

'Calling the hospital. I reckon he got caught up in some emergency. That'll be why his phone's going to voicemail.' Georgia held her phone to her ear. 'Hello. This is Georgia Bennett from the Outer Edinburgh Ambulance Service. Could you put me through to Dr Luke Anderson, please?'

The seconds ticked past. Kate could feel her heart thudding along with them. She leaned back against the headrest and closed her eyes. This turn of events was something she would never have expected and she wasn't at all sure how to deal with it.

She could hear the crackle of a voice coming back onto the other end of the line.

'Okay,' Georgia said, finally. 'Thank you. No, no message.'

She turned back to Kate who still had her eyes closed.

'The operator said he's unavailable for the rest of the day. On personal leave.'

Kate opened her eyes. She looked past the buildings around them. Up towards the walls of the castle.

'Where *is* he?' There was an angry edge to Georgia's voice now. 'How could he do something like this to you?'

A good question. Except that it was precisely what Kate had been about to do to him, wasn't it? She might not understand what was going on, but she couldn't put all the blame at Luke's feet. She blinked hard to keep tears at bay. Focussing on what she could see in the distance helped— that odd outline that created the kind of corners on the ramparts that she and Luke had discovered on their recent visit to Edinburgh castle.

Where they'd stood, looking out at that amazing view.

She could hear his words again, as clearly as

if he was leaning forward from the back seat of this car to whisper them in her ear.

I wonder how many people have stood in this spot and looked out at that view and tried to figure out what life is all about. Or what they really want from it.

'I think I might know where he is,' she said quietly.

'Good. Let's go and find him.' Georgia was scowling now. 'Oh, boy… I knew you can't trust men. Any of them. I actually thought Luke was different but now I can't wait to give him a piece of my mind.'

Kate smiled. 'I don't think so. What you can do is give me a lift to the top of the hill, though. Close to the castle gates?'

'You think he's gone sightseeing?'

'I don't know. It's just a hunch. But even if I don't find him, I could do with some time to think about things anyway.'

'Not by yourself, you don't. You need a friend right now.' Georgia started the car. 'I'll wait somewhere close for a while, okay? I don't care how long it takes. Text me when you need a ride home.' Her smile was sympathetic. 'I can buy chocolate and wine while I'm waiting.'

It helped to know that her best friend would be somewhere in the vicinity when Kate had purchased her ticket to tour the castle and went straight for the long flight of stairs that would take her up to the ramparts. If nothing else, she was going to get cold before too long. It might be a lovely, sunny day but there was enough of a breeze to ruffle the skirt of her dress and tease goose-bumps onto her bare arms.

Or maybe that was due to nerves.

She was running on instinct here, and it was quite possible she didn't know Luke as well as she thought she did. He could be miles away. Onto his third whisky in a bar somewhere perhaps. Feeling relieved that he'd dodged the bullet of committing himself to someone he couldn't really trust because she hadn't stuck to the premise of the pact?

He must have guessed somehow.

He had realised that she couldn't be trusted because she'd been hiding the truth.

Lying to him, even if it was only by omission.

This was a good thing, Kate told herself, rubbing at her arms as she kept walking. She would feel relieved to be able to be honest.

But…how devastating was it going to be to lose Luke?

She paused for a moment as the premonition of how much grief she was on the brink of became overwhelming.

Maybe she couldn't do this. It might be better to turn around and text Georgia to come back to the castle gates. To go and get that emergency supply of wine and chocolate and tissues and just go home and hide for a while.

And then she saw him.

Just a silhouette of a figure at this distance but she knew it was Luke. Not so much because it was obviously a tall, male shape but because it was in the exact spot that she had thought he might be. And because of how still he was standing, lost in the limitless view of those horizons that had made him ponder the meaning of life that most people had to deal with at some point. It was obviously his turn right now.

So Kate kept walking. It felt as though she was being pulled forward now, not pushing herself. As if she was within range of a magnetic force she couldn't resist. A force that became increasingly powerful with every step closing that distance between them.

And, as if he felt the same force, Luke turned away from the view by the time Kate was still metres away.

The colour seemed to drain from his face.

'*Katy...*'

He *was* wearing a suit and tie. He did look impossibly gorgeous. In a way, this was a comfort. Luke had obviously intended to go to the registry office. To marry her.

Whatever was going on, seeing her here was the last thing he'd expected, judging by how shocked he looked right now.

'Oh, my God... I only came here because I needed to think.' He wrenched at the sleeve of his jacket to expose his watch. 'I completely lost track of the time. We're so late…'

'Too late.' To her surprise, Kate's words sounded oddly calm. 'It's not going to happen now, Luke.'

He dropped his hands in slow motion and then his whole body seemed to freeze. Just a lock of that wavy brown hair got caught in the breeze and shifted on a furrowed forehead.

'You were waiting for me.' His voice cracked. 'You must have thought I'd changed my mind. That I wasn't coming…'

Kate shook her head. 'I couldn't go in,' she said, quietly. 'I couldn't do it.'

His face looked even paler now. His words came out in no more than a whisper. 'Why not?'

'Because I haven't been entirely honest with you. I broke the rules.' Kate wrapped her arms around herself as she shivered. 'I'm in love with you, Luke. I fell in love with you a long time ago.'

He didn't move a muscle. Even that stray lock of hair was completely still for a long, long moment.

But then one corner of his mouth moved, tilting upwards.

'That's okay,' he murmured. His whole body seemed to be waking up now. He was taking a step towards her.

It was Kate's turn to freeze. It was *okay*? He didn't mind that she had broken the most important rule? What was going on here?

'I broke that rule, too.' The warmth of Luke's hands on her bare arms was startling. Almost as astonishing as what she was hearing. 'I'm in love with you, too. Oh, Katy… I love you *so* much…'

His hands had moved to cradle her face and the touch was gentle. The touch of his lips on hers was gentle as well. Heartbreakingly tender.

And this kiss was different from any kiss they had shared before.

Because it was honest?

Because it was possible to let every ounce of the love she felt for this man rush through her body and be communicated through what was only a tiny patch of physical contact?

Maybe it was because she was receiving the

exact same kind of message. She could sense the power of a love that matched her own and together they were fusing into something extraordinary.

Kate never wanted this kiss to end. It was only a lack of enough oxygen that finally forced her to pull back far enough to snatch a gasp of breath.

The breeze had picked up again. She could feel her skirt swirling around her legs and strands of her hair were blowing over her face to snag on moist lips. Luke smoothed them away, his gaze locked on hers.

Kate never wanted that eye contact to end either. How amazing was it that love could be felt as a physical force by the touch of a gaze as much as lips?

So powerful, it sent a shudder through her entire body.

'You're cold.' A furrow appeared between Luke's eyes. He shrugged off his suit jacket and draped it over Kate's shoulders. The smooth silk of the lining kissed her skin and the warmth that had come from Luke's body wrapped itself around her like an even more intimate caress.

For a moment, Kate was transported back to that memorable night when they had agreed to reinstate the pact. When she'd been engulfed by his oversized anorak and had caught the scent of Luke from its soft, woolly lining. She'd been under the erotic spell of those first waves of intense, physical desire for this man that night.

That spell had never worn off. If anything, it felt stronger now. A part of her life instead of just a temporary sprinkle of magic dust.

Luke took hold of her hand. 'Come on, let's find somewhere out of this wind.'

It didn't matter that there were tourists everywhere in the castle grounds. It felt as if she and Luke were the only people in the world. And when they went into the first sheltered building they could find, miraculously they *were* the only people in the space.

They tucked themselves into a corner of one of the few wooden pews in the ancient chapel of St Margaret's in front of its carved stone archway with the soft glow of the small, stained-glass window behind the altar on the other side of the archway.

It seemed entirely appropriate to celebrate the discovery of this new level of love by sharing another kiss.

And by speaking only in whispers.

'When?' Luke asked. 'When did *you* break the rules?'

'That first night we had dinner. At that Italian restaurant?' Kate had to smile. 'Just before you said how much better it was just to be friends and how you could never trust being in love. When you persuaded me to give the pact a go.'

Luke groaned softly. 'I did say that, didn't I? I actually believed it.'

'I couldn't tell you. Not after that. I was too scared you might disappear from my life. Because you couldn't trust me.'

'I could never *not* trust you, Katy. I'm trusting you with my heart for ever now. With my life…'

'But I was being untrustworthy. I was lying. Pretending that I felt the same way you did.'

Luke's smile was ironic. 'You did a good job, too. You were so good I believed you so well that I couldn't tell you how I really felt. In case *you* disappeared.'

'When did you know?'

'That night you got hit by the car. When I thought the worst for a few seconds and realised how much I didn't want to live without you. But you know what?'

'What?'

'I think I'd actually felt that way for ever. I just hadn't realised what had been hiding.'

Kate nodded. 'Do you want to know something else? When we first met, way back at med school, I…um…had a real crush on you.'

'What? *Really?* How come I never knew that?'

'I could see the way you looked at other girls. I felt kind of invisible in that way. I guess I got good at hiding it and then I convinced myself I was over it.'

'I must have been completely blind,' Luke groaned. 'Or maybe I just needed to grow up enough to see what was real and what wasn't.'

He shook his head sadly. 'We've wasted a lot of time, haven't we?'

Kate mirrored the headshake. 'It wasn't wasted. If that's what was needed to get us to where we are right now, I'd do it again in a heartbeat.'

'I'm sorry about the registry office. It might be a long time before we can get a new appointment.'

'It doesn't matter.'

Luke kissed her before he spoke again. 'It *does* matter. And it doesn't seem enough any more. My first wedding was in a registry office. I think I want a *real* wedding this time.'

'With me in a meringue dress and people throwing rose petals?'

'Whatever spins your wheels.' Luke smiled. 'But, yes, I want it to be a bit over the top. With all our friends here to witness it. In a really special place.' He turned his head to gaze around them. 'Like this…'

'You probably have to book years in advance to get a wedding in this chapel.'

'We got lucky with the registry office. People cancel sometimes, you know.'

'Or they don't turn up.' Kate's smile was teasing. 'I wonder how often it happens that *both* people don't turn up to their own wedding?'

'That wouldn't work. We'd need at least a bit of time. So that you can buy the meringue.'

'I don't want a meringue. But… I *do* want a real wedding.' A bubble of excitement was layering itself onto the sheer joy of knowing that Luke loved her this much. That he was *in* love with her. The dreams of the future were within touching distance now. Maybe the dreams from the past could be indulged a little, too.

A sacred place. A white dress. Heartfelt pledges made in front of others. A slow walk down an aisle because every step would bring her closer to the man she loved.

Closer to the rest of her life with Luke.

'You know what?'

'What?'

'It wouldn't hurt to *ask*…'

* * *

The evening chill in the air wasn't entirely responsible for the shivery sensation that rippled down Kate's spine.

'What if he's not there?'

Georgie snorted. 'As if...'

She cast a critical eye over Kate's dress. The bead-encrusted lace bodice had a sweetheart neckline in the front and a deep V at the back. From just under the bust, a drape of pale, ivory silk fell far enough to touch the cobbles of this courtyard.

'Phew... I thought for sure you were going to get some marks on that skirt climbing those stairs.'

'I was being careful. What about my hair? There's enough of a breeze up here to have messed with it.'

'You look stunning.' Georgia's smile was misty. 'And I love that wreath. The flowers are so tiny.'

'You look pretty amazing yourself, Georgie.'

'For a bridesmaid the size of a small elephant, you mean?' Georgia ran her hands over her belly.

'Thank goodness for wraparound dress styles. I feel more elegant than I have for months.'

Kate drew in a shaky breath. 'This is really happening, isn't it?'

'It would seem so. I can't believe you're doing it here, though. At the *castle*.'

'I *know*. Who knew that some American couple was going to have a last-minute hitch with their visas? Or that we happened to make an enquiry on the only day ever that St Margaret's chapel didn't have a waiting list for cancellations?'

Everything had simply fallen into place after that. Finding the perfect dress in the first shop she and Georgia had gone into. Job interviews in New Zealand that fitted perfectly into the timeframe for an extended honeymoon.

'And you got the whole package. The party in that tower next door afterwards. Even the piper to serenade your walk up the aisle. Oh, look… I think that's him getting ready.' Georgia sighed happily. 'I do love a man in a kilt.'

Kate eyed the stone archway that was the entrance to the tiny chapel. She could see the soft light beyond that would be coming from the dozens of candles. The pews would be filled with the twenty or so close friends who had been chosen to witness this ceremony. Through the internal archway, in the space at the front beside the altar, would be where Luke was standing.

Waiting for her.

Some muffled squeaking sounds were coming from the direction of the lone piper as he got his bagpipes ready.

'Stand by...' Georgia said in a stage whisper.

'No...' The call came from behind them. *'Wait...'*

Both Georgia and Kate turned swiftly to see a figure running towards them. A tall, dark man in a dark suit, a black bow-tie against a snowy, white shirt.

For the briefest moment Kate thought it was Luke, arriving late to his own wedding. But then her face lit up with the widest smile.

'*Matteo*...you made it.'

'I didn't think I could. Not after the last delay with the fog.' Matteo was out of breath. 'But I couldn't let my best friend get married without me.' He put his hand to his chest as he tried to catch his breath. 'You look...*bellissima*, Kate. Luke is a very lucky man.'

'He certainly is,' Georgia put in. 'Hi, Matteo.' The glance she slid towards Kate was oddly accusatory. 'You didn't tell me Matteo was coming.'

'We really weren't sure that he could make it. Luke's going to be as surprised as you.'

But probably happier.

Was that why Kate hadn't mentioned the idea of flying in the only option for a best man? There'd been something between Georgia and Matteo back at the competition. Something that hadn't ended so well despite her friend's refusal to ever discuss it. Just how acrimonious had it been when Matteo had been discarded in favour of Dave the New Zealander—the man she still suspected might be the father of Georgia's babies?

She could see the shocked expression on Matteo's face as his gaze slid over Georgia's impressive bump.

He cleared his throat. 'Hello, Georgia. You're looking…um…well?'

'I'm very well, thank you.'

'I'd better get inside. Give me a minute to find my place, okay?' Matteo disappeared through the arched entrance just as the piper finished warming up and began to play.

'Here we go,' Georgia said. 'You good?'

Her smile was bright. If Matteo's presence wasn't something she wanted, she wasn't about to let it interfere with Kate's special day. She'd make sure she found time to talk to her closest friend later. To let her know how much she was loved and how much Kate appreciated everything she'd done to help her through the last few weeks.

'Never better.' She nodded. 'I feel like I've been waiting for this moment my whole life.'

'It was always going to happen. I knew you were fated to find your perfect person.'

'But I'd never have dreamed it would be Luke.'

'You can thank me, later.' Georgia touched

Kate's arm and nodded towards the entrance. 'It's time, hon.'

But Kate hesitated a moment longer. 'It *was* down to you, wasn't it? It was your idea to go that competition. We might never have reconnected otherwise. I hope...well... I hope I can return the favour one day.'

Georgia shook her head, a stray curl escaping from the pins holding her hair in place.

'No, thanks. Just make sure *you* live happily ever after, okay?'

'I'll do my best.'

The sound of the bagpipes would have been overpowering in the small space of the chapel but, drifting in behind them, the haunting notes were beautiful.

Of course Luke was there. With Matteo on one side of him and the minister waiting on the other side. The pews were full but Luke was only looking at one person.

At *her*.

And that gaze was drawing her forward so

compellingly it was hard to remember to walk slowly.

This was it. Her dream wedding. To the only person she could imagine wanting it to be with.

Luke was smiling at her as she got closer. A smile that was full of joy. Brimming with love…

Kate smiled back but she knew it was wobbly.

Her heart felt too full and her eyes were going to follow its example any moment. She could feel those tears of pure joy gathering.

Because she wasn't going to be alone in doing her best to live happily ever after, was she?

She had found her partner for life.

* * * * *

LET'S TALK

Romance

For exclusive extracts, competitions
and special offers, find us online:

f facebook.com/millsandboon

📷 @millsandboonuk

🐦 @millsandboon

Or get in touch on 0844 844 1351*

For all the latest titles coming soon,
visit millsandboon.co.uk/nextmonth

Want even more
ROMANCE?

Join our bookclub today!